Attracted as she wa... afraid to trust him.

"I'm afraid you'll have to ... ous. In fact I'd like to be very truthful with you always. I mean truthful regarding my feelings. I've never had that freedom with anyone."

"I did. Once."

"With your mother?"

"How did you know?"

"Franklin told me."

"How is it you two are such friends?"

"Who can explain friendship but God? Who can explain the friendship between Jonathan and David? Or...you and me." He touched her hand. This time she didn't withdraw.

"Is that what it is? Friendship?"

"We best call it that for now."

For now? she thought. *And what was later?*

The buggy was spinning. She felt short of breath. She tilted her head back and closed her eyes. If only a breeze would cool her face. She felt dizzy. Soft warmth smothered her lips. No. It couldn't be. No man had ever done that to her. Was this her first kiss? She opened her eyes. Yes, he was kissing her! Her head was swimming. She felt like she was melting. She wanted him to hold her. She would do anything to keep that moment. She pulled away from him. Or had he pulled away from her? She didn't know. She had never felt so dizzy. No, it was giddy. No, it was ecstasy. Rapture. At last she knew real passion. She was afraid to open her eyes. What would she say now?

ROBIN CHANDLER is an author from Kansas who uses a pseudonym. *Love in the Prairie Wilds* is Robin's first **Heartsong Presents** title.

Love
in the Prairie Wilds

Robin Chandler

Heartsong Presents

*With much gratitude to the love of my life,
whose patience and faith sustain me.*

A note from the Author:
*I love to hear from my readers! You may write to me at
the following address:*   **Robin Chandler
Author Relations
P.O. Box 719
Uhrichsville, OH 44683**

ISBN 1-55748-709-X

LOVE IN THE PRAIRIE WILDS

Cover illustration by Brian Bowman.

PRINTED IN THE U.S.A.

one

Holly Bennington trembled. Did she hear the hardwood floors creaking outside the door? Why had she been told to come here right out of her etiquette class at the Gladwyne School for Young Ladies?

Her anxiety gnawed on her. Did it mean she didn't trust God? Surely God would forgive her. It seemed like only yesterday she had waited and trembled on this same hard chair in Headmistress Snade's office. It seemed like only yesterday that Mrs. Snade walked in and broke Holly's heart with news that Papa died from an attack of appendicitis.

Why did things have to change?

The creaking hardwood grew louder and louder.

"Oh no. Please. Not again," she gasped as she stared at the doorknob. "Oh, Lord, spare my brother Franklin. He's all the family I have left."

The door knob turned.

Mrs. Snade entered. "Oh, Miss Bennington—"

"It's my brother Franklin!" cried Holly.

"Sit up straight! Look me in the eye! Speak in a modest, yet distinctly audible tone!"

"Yes, ma'am," answered Holly correctly.

"That's better, Miss Bennington."

"Is my brother dead?"

"Heavens, no. He wrote me a letter."

"Oh, thank God for that."

"You must always be thankful to God, regardless of good news or bad news."

"I was worried. He's some kind of soldier way out on the frontier somewhere."

5

"Precision please, Miss Bennington. This is 1877. We have a new president." Mrs. Snade clasped her hands on her desk. Every bony knuckle grew white as frost as she waited for Holly to acknowledge the lithograph of a long-bearded man on the wall behind her.

"President Rutherford Hayes?" guessed Holly.

"Yes." Mrs. Snade almost smiled. "A woman's lot is hard, Miss Bennington. We can't vote. We can't hold public office. We are hooted down if we dare speak in public. If we're married we have no rights to property or even our own children. But we must never give up. We must be very brave!" Mrs. Snade slammed her hands down on the desk. "Perhaps you should find out *what kind* of soldier your brother is. Perhaps you should find out *where* he is."

"He doesn't write much," Holly answered dryly. Now that she knew Franklin was safe, resentment simmered inside her again. He hadn't even come back for Papa's funeral. He had been out on a winter campaign, whatever that was.

Mrs. Snade scowled. "When he does write, as is evidenced by this letter, his letters are short—but hardly usable as models of brevity because they are also awkward and barely legible."

"I'm sorry."

"I'm afraid, however, that it is not my purpose to critique your brother's letter but to inform you what facts were written therein. The central fact is that your late father's estate does not have funds adequate to maintain your continued attendance at our school."

Holly gasped, "I must leave Gladwyne School?"

"Precisely."

What would she do? Perhaps she could get a job as a governess or maybe even as a teacher. Yes, she must use her education. She had heard such awful stories about young ladies cutting fabric and sewing garments for terrible factories in New York City. She could never do that!

"Am I too young to get a decent job?" she murmured.

"Nineteen? Youth is not your problem, Miss Bennington. Anyway it won't be necessary to find a job. In the letter, your brother sent you a ticket and some expense money. You are to go by train to live with him in the desolation called Nebraska. With patience, even there you will find a young gentle—a young man worthy of matrimony. Your brother will meet you when the train stops momentarily at…at…" Mrs. Snade's eyes skimmed the letter until they soured in distaste. "At a place called Sidney."

Holly arose in a daze. "Thank you, Headmistress Snade."

"Speak distinctly! Stand tall. Heavens, you're short enough as you are."

Holly's good-byes to friends at Gladwyne School rushed by in a tearful blur. This was all so sudden. She had so much on her mind. How could she live with her bachelor brother in the wilderness? What would she do there? Was she once again to become the forgotten lady in the household—with no authority, no responsibility, and worse yet, maybe no future?

But she might be wrong. Did they have socials on the frontier? She was almost old enough to wear real bonnets instead of hats, and long dangly earrings instead of dainties. Were the shops there full of the latest bonnets and fashions?

Holly soon discovered that she couldn't move back into the family home at Fairmont Park. The family lawyer refused to see Holly but sent her a letter that began by politely explaining he had at Franklin's request directed the family butler to discretely store a few keepsakes. Everything else was auctioned, including the house, to pay a portion of Papa's debts, Holly's last school bill, and small pittances to the dismissed family servants. The lawyer not so politely pointed out that he had performed services for Gideon Bennington and his family far too long already without collecting his normal fees. He no longer served the Bennington family. In the future Holly should let her brother handle matters like any proper young lady would.

"So even the law thinks Franklin is right to make every decision for me!"

Holly felt an anger she had never known before. She tore at the letter. She would never go west unless she was absolutely destitute. Once out west she would really be Franklin's prisoner.

She used the expense money Franklin sent her to move into the Betsy Ross Hotel in downtown Philadelphia, determined to find a job teaching. From there she began to visit schools in the area.

She reasoned that the month of May was a very good time of the year to look. Few jobs had been contracted for the following school year. Yet she couldn't find a job. More than one school superintendent, after interviewing Holly and consulting Headmistress Snade, wrote a letter to Holly hinting she might be too timid to discipline children. But every superintendent in every school consoled her by writing in his rejection letter that there were many jobs out west. They were desperate for teachers of any kind!

Finding work as a governess was just as unsuccessful. Once again, prospective employers hinted Holly might be too timid to handle active children. That's when she began to suspect persnickety Mrs. Snade, anxious to protect the glorious name of Gladwyne, was not recommending her for employment. Holly would never find a job!

But she had not exhausted her last hope: Granville Wiggins III.

He was the only young man who had called on her at the school more than once. But to his credit, since her papa's death he had sat with her in the school parlor every couple of weeks or so. She thought of him as her beau—although she was careful not to tell anyone else that.

Hope swelled within Holly as she paused in front of a two-story, white-frame colonial in Cheltenham on the outskirts of Philadelphia. She had never done such a bold thing before.

Her knees quaked under her bombazine dress. To emphasize her gloom she wore the only black dress she owned. She had already removed its gay cherry streamers for Papa's funeral.

The iron gate was open, so she had no excuse not to walk to the massive front door. Her dress rustled around her laced shoes in the silence. Her right fist, gloved in pale gray kid, seemed too weak and shaky to knock. She had to grip her wrist with her left hand and force a rap on the door.

"Holly!" Granville Wiggins III greeted her with a walrus-mustached smile and a warm damp handshake. "I was going to call on you today." He frowned. "Now why didn't the maid answer the door?" He remembered to smile again. Granville was slightly breathless. He was usually slightly breathless. "How did you get here?"

"By hackney cab."

"All the way from the school?" He waved her into the parlor.

"I'm staying at the Betsy Ross Hotel."

"You've left Gladwyne School?" His eyes narrowed even more than usual.

"Yes."

"Please sit down. Tea? But of course." He pulled a cord on the wall. "Mother is out. I'm sure she would be delighted to meet you. I'm sorry I haven't seen you for a while. But business has swamped me lately. And the business of a Wiggins is business, then more business."

Granville tugged some slack at the knees of his black wool pants as he sat down. He arranged his black wool jacket, then laughed but not heartily enough to make his monocle pop out of his eye. Even Holly, in spite of her usual self-conscious preoccupation, had noticed he was very embarrassed when that happened. His monocle did not bother her at all. His face was handsome with a prominent chin and strong aquiline nose. It didn't bother her that he tilted his head back so that his nostrils flared and punctuated his every sentence. And it certainly didn't bother her that his conversations usually centered on money—not today anyway!

"Holly, you're silent as a clam, as usual." He seemed to realize he had been indelicate. "But who wouldn't be silent after losing their father? After all, I lost my own father two short years ago. And how it changed my life!" Granville studied her. White sausage fingers groped for each other and intertwined over his vest. "But I see more than grief in your eyes. Has something else happened?"

"That's so perceptive, Granville." This was the moment she was waiting for. She must tell her story truthfully and appealingly, while avoiding any sign of self-pity. "It's father's estate. Apparently there is a snag regarding funds."

"Tied up? But who would be contesting his will, my dear? Your wandering brother? Where is that maid?" He ran his hand through coarse black hair that waved straight back. He was proud of his hair.

"Not tied up so much exactly."

"I can well imagine a huge brick factory like your father owned could have some encumbrances. Just nuisances no doubt." He frowned when she didn't react, then glanced uneasily toward a double door leading back into the house. Holly guessed a maid should have entered those double doors by now. Granville stood up slowly and reached for the cord.

She proceeded cautiously, "Yes. Well, I'm not familiar with the account books myself but apparently there is a problem with my funding."

"And the school won't extend you some credit?" Doubt flickered across his pink face. He didn't pull the cord.

"No. They won't. You see I've only been at the school a year and a half. Before that I was privately tutored."

"Is that relevant?" His face pouted, then reddened. "Is it possible that this lack of funds may be more than a temporary situation, my dear?"

"Yes."

"Good grief! There's no money?"

"Not now it seems." She added carelessly, "I was hoping to get a small loan so I could—"

"No money? Bennington Brickworks is broke?" Granville's eyes genuinely mourned. "No money ever?"

"Probably not." She added forcefully, "I was hoping to get a small loan so I could—"

"What about your father's wealthy acquaintances?"

"What a bright, sensitive question!" Holly smiled bravely. "You see, Granville, poor grieving Papa completely withdrew from society after Mama's death. Maybe that was why he kept me in the house too long. Papa was so lonely. And he worked late almost every night on business. Anyway, after eight years of that isolation, even his friends forgot us. Otherwise, I'm sure his wealthy friends in the club he once frequented would be standing in line right now, clamoring to be my benefactors. "So," she articulated slowly, "I was hoping to get a small loan so I could—"

"Doesn't your church practice charity?" he muttered lifelessly.

She must revive his sagging interest. She batted her eyes and spoke louder, "That's so discerning of you, Granville. But poor distraught Papa not only abandoned the church after Mama's passing, but I'm afraid in his grief he was also rude to the pastors who came to console us! Of course, you know I couldn't attend services alone. I was only a young girl. If all that hadn't happened, supportive pastors would surround me on every side this very moment." She put on her brightest, perkiest smile. She rattled rapidly, "If I could get a small loan I would have time to look for work!"

"Small loan?" He mumbled, "Well, we all have our money problems."

"If I can't find work," she sputtered desperately, "I'll have to go west to live with my brother. And of course you don't want me to disappear in the distant wilds."

"That's probably best," he mumbled sadly. He pulled a gold watch from his watch pocket. "Dear me. I just remembered, Miss Bennington. I have an appointment at my bank."

A plump, gray-haired woman in an elegant dark maroon dress paused at the double door and peered into the room. She didn't look like a maid. She said, "I just got back from the bank." Her face was flush with disappointment. She asked anxiously, "Are you interviewing for a new maid, Granville? I thought we decided we couldn't—"

"Excuse me," snapped Granville, drowning out the woman's voice, "but Miss Bennington must leave."

At the front door Holly reminded him, "I'm at the Betsy Ross Hotel, Granville. If I could just get a small loan—" The front door closed in her face before she could finish.

In a cloud of confusion, she found a cab. As the horse clopped toward her hotel, her anger grew. She felt hurt and foolish too. To think she had planned to ask for a small loan—not *if* but *when* Granville Wiggins III proposed! What now? Should she slave in the garment industry in New York City? Or should she waste her precious life in the wilderness? In her heart she knew she would have to choose the lesser evil: brother Franklin. Oh what a desperate end she had come to!

At the Betsy Ross Hotel, she paced her tiny room made as snug as a mouse's den by her encroaching wardrobe. Stacked high were hat boxes with small perky hats of every fabric, suitable for a young lady of promise for every season and every level of polite society. She had mounds of dresses of muslin and taffeta and watered silk and velvet and satin-tiered dresses festooned with lace, sashes, nets, ribbons, billows, and ruffles. They made a slight young lady look wonderfully robust. They were dyed rich reds, blues, browns, and plums. But the greens! The greens exhausted description: verdigris, frog green, moss green, sage green, canary green, bottle green, sea green, and a dozen more! Such splendor required never-seen petticoats, pantalets, and corsets. Holly even had a handful of everyday dresses from calicos and poplins somewhere in the mounds.

"Poor Papa," she said as she weaved through her clothes. "How he spoiled me with pretties. And no one ever came to call on me a second time but Granville Wiggins III." She laughed, startled by her note of hysteria.

Day after day she paced the room, waiting for a school superintendent to offer her a teaching job, waiting for a family to hire her as their nanny, waiting for Granville Wiggins III to realize his wonderful Holly was really leaving and to breathlessly call on her. She had forgiven him. After all, he was just stunned and momentarily rude. Was his awkwardness any worse than her own?

Meanwhile, the money Holly received from brother Franklin dwindled away. She bought more time by exchanging Franklin's ticket for the finest hotel car available on the train for a new ticket on the cheapest passenger car available on the train and cash. But as surely as sights and sounds of day and night alternated relentlessly on the street outside her tiny window, that cash dwindled away, too.

Finally, one morning she walked solemnly the few blocks to a cemetery near Christ Church. "Gideon" was etched fresh next to "Rachel" on the Bennington stone towering over the graves of Papa and Mama. Two small headstones marked the burial sites of baby brother Noah and baby sister Rebecca—both born before Holly. Mama had been dead for a long time too. Could it be eight years? Holly wept and prayed over the graves.

That same morning Holly boarded the train.

two

"May I sit anywhere?" Holly timidly asked the black-uniformed conductor for the Pennsylvania Railroad. She lugged a wicker basket in one hand and a carpet bag in the other.

He smirked at the basket. "Just so you don't eat all that picnic in somebody's lap."

What did he mean by that? Holly sniffed and hastily sat down on a hard bench seat by the window.

She waited until she stopped shaking, then removed the epidote-studded pin that secured her tiny-brimmed hat of lemon-green velvet. She placed the hat on the wicker basket beside her, careful not to crumple the long yellow satin ribbons. Her fingers flitted over laced tiers of her mustard-green dress, smoothing them like small graceful birds tidying a nest. The muslin dress, gathered up bulkily behind her, made leaning back uncomfortable, but she endured it. It was the style.

The train lurched and picked up speed. When the light was just right, Holly saw her reflection in the window instead of streaming trees and houses. Her hair was parted in the middle and pulled back above her ears. Long tresses were braided and pinned up behind her head in two thick loops. She hadn't crimped her bangs today. Nor had she made any delightful finger puffs. Her hair was burnished walnut, with just enough red to look wonderful with greens.

But her hair was only a frame for her face. Her skin was clear and white as ivory. So she was lucky. It was not proper to wear powder or rouge. She was sure her face was pleasant—even sweet—with dark eyebrows almost black and a slightly concave nose. Her ears were the tiniest white china saucers. And they had to be exposed. It was the fashion. So she was

14

lucky. Her chin was passably strong. Her forehead was wide and intelligent.

What concerned her about the reflection was the lack of resolution. The face was unsure, devoid of toughness. She was certain if she could see her eyes they would be radiant—adorable papa said—but scared, the glowing brown eyes of a frightened rabbit. Papa had sheltered her too long. He should have sent her to Gladwyne School years before he did. Perhaps she could will a change. Or she could pretend until she got so used to the change, it became real. She was good at pretending. She would pretend to be like Headmistress Snade. A lady couldn't be more purposeful than Mrs. Snade.

"Do you have a ticket, missy?" It was the conductor. His face wore an ugly smirk again. "Are you really old enough to dress up in your mama's clothes?"

Holly took a deep breath and pretended she was Mrs. Snade. She felt her lips trembling. She was so scared. And she couldn't ask God to help her be mean.

"My age is no concern of yours, sir!" She pulled the ticket from her purse and made him bend over to take it.

"Thank you, ma'am," he said uncertainly.

"You are most welcome, Mister…." She forced herself to pointedly stare at his name plate. "Harris, is it?"

She watched him move on down the aisle taking tickets. She felt very sick inside. Hot and cool at the same time. She was quivering too. But her new resolve had squelched the conductor very effectively. Her new toughness seemed most appropriate for dealing with disrespectful ruffians. And the west was sure to be brimming over with them.

Every few minutes it seemed, a young man entered the car hawking apples, oranges, and pears, then newspapers, then sandwiches, then cigars, then grapes, then peanuts—none of which Holly could buy even if she wanted to. If the young man looked at her more than one second, she scorched him with a glare that would wither the leaves off an oak tree.

It was very hot even for early June, so windows on the coach had to be lowered during the afternoon to get fresh air. Every so often, sulfury coal smoke from the engine billowed inside and gagged her. But that evening when the windows were closed again, new smells tormented her. The men in the car smelled as if they hadn't bathed in weeks.

Rest was rare, sleep nearly impossible. From the wicker basket at her side she nibbled hard-boiled eggs, pickles, sausage, and hard bread the hotel had packed for her. That evening the train stopped in Pittsburgh. The next morning as Holly refreshed herself in the lady's dressing room, nothing moved past the window but forest and a few open meadows. The train rolled into Chicago in the afternoon. She not only changed trains but railroads. Now she rode the Rock Island. For the first time she began to worry about the rest of her luggage. She had checked it into the baggage car in Philadelphia.

Rolling fields of tall grass waved past her window. At noon the next day she switched railroads again. From Omaha she rode the Union Pacific. How could her bags ever find her? She had never been so miserable. Would the trip west ever end? That afternoon she used her one change of clothes, adorning herself in a plum skirt and otter brown jacket. Once again the landscape changed. It was now flat, treeless prairie. She endured a long sleepless night of clacking rails and creepy silent stops for water and coal.

Exactly sixty-seven hours after she boarded the train in Philadelphia, she pinned on a small perky calling hat of plum velvet and long satin streamers and stepped down into the crisp dawn at Sidney. She was so numb from lack of sleep she could hardly appreciate the sight of men hurriedly unloading her belongings from the baggage car and stacking them neatly on the depot platform.

A black-uniformed man approached her. "I'm the station master, ma'am. Are you Holly Bennington?"

"Yes, I am."

"Wait here, please." He jogged down the platform and stopped where men seemed to be loading long crates into a wagon. The rising sun blinded her. Minutes later he returned. "We'll have you fixed up here real quick. Excuse me, ma'am, but I've got to get back to the telegraph."

Holly watched her train depart. Looking west was easy on tired eyes. Soon she couldn't even see the black cloud billowing from the train's smokestack. She heard boots behind her.

A red-bearded man in a wide-brimmed tan hat sauntered over to her. "That's a dandy outfit, ma'am, but—"

"I don't speak to strangers, sir. If you don't leave me alone, I'll scream for the station master."

"Whew! I just talked to the station master. He said Lieutenant Bennington's sister was young and thin as a stick. He didn't say anything about salty manners. Are you Miss Bennington or not, ma'am?"

"Just who are you, sir?"

"I'm Jonah Finch. The station master asked me to take Miss Holly Bennington to Lieutenant Bennington."

She nodded coldly at the man. "I'm Miss Bennington. You may take my luggage."

"Which one is yours, ma'am?"

"All of them, sir."

She watched him stride to a large freight wagon parked near the platform. He yanked back a tarpaulin that covered long wooden crates. He loaded her seventeen bags, eleven cardboard boxes and one wicker basket on top of the crates, then covered everything with the tarpaulin again. He worked fast as he whistled "Barbara Allen." He was sinewy and taller than the wagon wheels, which she guessed were six feet high. His shoulders were broad under a white cotton shirt. Buckskin pants were tucked into rawhide boots. On his belt a holster held a large ivory-handled knife.

"Did I forget anything?" he asked, perhaps smiling under the thick beard.

"Just me," she might have joked airily if he had been a gentleman who knew only old men wore long beards these days.

Instead she asked coldly, "Am I to ride on that monstrosity, sir?"

He answered by helping her climb up to the high seat of the freight wagon. The huge wagon was pulled by four stout black mules. She glanced back to see a rangy horse tied to the back of the wagon. Its coat was glossy reddish brown. Its mane and tail were shimmering black. Papa had taught Holly enough about riding to know it was well-groomed.

"Do you like my old bay, ma'am?"

"I'm not in the habit of disliking horses, sir."

As the freight wagon rumbled along the main street of Sidney raising a cloud of dust, a handful of white frame buildings yielded to many buildings of rough, fresh-cut pine. Some of these structures were long and low, like barracks. A corral milled with horses and mules. Bags were piled in neat stacks. They must be approaching Franklin's quarters.

The man was now whistling "Jimmy Crack Corn." The ride in the wagon jolted Holly's perky hat askew. She saw her shadow against a building. Her long streamers bounced crazily. She must have looked like a fool. She would be so glad when they stopped at Franklin's. A hot cup of tea would be nice. And then she would retire for a nap. She had hardly slept for three days. When she woke up refreshed she would explain politely to Franklin that she was going to catch the next train east. She wouldn't tell him she was going to slave in the garment industry in New York City.

Now nothing lay ahead of the wagon but treeless prairie. She didn't like to speak to this red-bristled roughneck but she had to. "Didn't you see those barracks back there? Take me to my brother Franklin."

He stopped whistling, let the heavy wagon roll to a stop and held the reins loosely in thick rough hands. He acted as if he wanted to gawk at her but had to hold his head to keep staring straight ahead. "Are you serious, ma'am?"

"Of course I am serious, mister."

"Those are called the Sidney Barracks. Didn't the lieutenant write you that he is stationed in Camp Robinson?"

"As a matter of fact, he did. So where is the camp?"

"Ma'am, I want you to know that I'm serious now. Camp Robinson is up yonder to the north. There's nothing between this spot right here and Camp Robinson but one or two curious prairie dogs and over a hundred miles of buffalo grass!"

"One hundred miles! How long will the trip take?"

"I reckon it will take until sometime in the afternoon—"

"Afternoon! That long? That's intolerable."

"Sometime in the afternoon tomorrow."

"Tomorrow! Am I to spend the night with…with a strange man on the trail?"

"No, ma'am. We'll spend the night at a station between the Platte River and Camp Robinson. A station is where folks can water and rest their horses and mules."

Holly was struck by horrifying doubt. "Prove my brother asked you to do this!"

What if he couldn't prove it? Should she jump off the wagon? Would he then ride off with her every possession if she did? What was his name again? Job Fisk? Or John Fisk?

The man laughed through the thick red beard. "You are cautious, aren't you? That's good I reckon." He fished a letter from his shirt pocket. "The station master gave this letter to me back there when I was loading my goods."

Holly held the letter with trembling hands. The scrawl was definitely inked by Franklin. Yes, the letter asked whoever happened to be freighting supplies to the camp the day Miss Holly Bennington arrived on the train to please bring her, too. There was a hint of exasperation in the letter.

She turned her anger on the man. "Franklin didn't exactly ask you in particular, did he?"

"No, ma'am. He sure didn't."

"If I'm going to cross this wasteland under the boiling sun I must find a proper summer hat and a parasol."

As she directed his search into her sea of boxes and luggage she reflected how Franklin had entrusted her to a complete stranger. How could Franklin be so insensitive? By the time she found a hat and a parasol, she was fuming. The floppy wide-brimmed hat was white straw with a long red ostrich feather. The frilly parasol was pink. They didn't match her outfit—or each other.

She withdrew under her mismatched protection. As the wagon rumbled along in two ruts worn deep into the trail she smoldered for a long time about etiquette of the frontier. She didn't dare ask about sleeping accommodations at the station between the Platte River and Camp Robinson. The answer might be too frightening.

The man tugged on gloves and whistled "Listen to the Mockingbird" over and over. Holly found herself despising his rough unfinished leather boots propped on the front rail of the floorboard, then despising his rough unfinished leather gloves holding the long reins, then his boots again, then his gloves again. That was this man all right: unfinished. But she kept watching him anyway. The breeze brought her a rich grass smell. She couldn't bring herself to watch the rippling prairie; she might start liking it.

Once in a while the man wordlessly offered her a canteen and she was too thirsty to refuse. The water had the sharp taste and smell of metal. Water spilled on her jacket each time the wagon lurched.

She had to look up once to see what was making a commotion. A grim-faced rider on a huge buckskin horse waved his hat and blistered past them in the opposite direction. Lathered sweat flaked off the buckskin.

"Somebody must be chasing him!" she gasped.

"No, ma'am. He's a mail rider from Camp Robinson. Taking mail to the railroad depot at Sidney."

Her hands shook so much she had to grip the parasol with both hands to steady them. "Can't we go any faster?"

"I could if I changed my team every fifteen miles or so like a stagecoach driver does. But I only have one team, ma'am."

Hours later, buttes grew on the northern horizon. "That's

Chimney Rock. That's Courthouse Rock," grunted the unfinished man. He resumed whistling "Little Brown Jug."

"Illuminating," muttered Holly. She didn't know what irritated her more: his whistling, the constant jolts, or the searing breeze. She wasn't pretending to be Headmistress Snade any more. She realized she preferred to never think about Mrs. Snade again.

Inside the red beard the man's face may have smiled. "The Platte River is down there."

Water ribboned across the prairie. The Platte was like no river Holly had ever seen before. It was wide and shallow, choked with sand. Long narrow sandbars emerged out in the middle of the river. Black forms moved along the water's edge.

"Buffalo?" she asked no one in particular.

"Right, ma'am. The Platte River has good hunting."

"Why didn't the Army build the camp there?"

"The Sioux are up north."

"How do you spell that? Are you talking about a tribe of Indians?"

"Yes, ma'am."

Reality crawled over Holly like a spider suddenly recognized for what it is. Her voice was high. "Do you mean the camp is inside some kind of reservation for the Sioux Indians?"

"It's called Red Cloud's Agency, ma'am."

Holly shuddered. "How many of these Sioux are in the reservation?"

"That's what the Army has been trying to find out for a long time. The Sioux don't want the Army to know exactly how many. That way they can come and go as they please. But I reckon most of the time there's about ten thousand."

"Ten thousand!"

How could matters get worse? And she had worried about the danger in the garment industry! How could she have been so foolish as to come west? What was her brother Franklin thinking about? Had his brain cracked and moldered in this dry hot oven of a wilderness?

Before they reached the Platte, the wagon clattered across a pebbly creek. "Punkinseed Creek." The man laughed.

"What is so funny about pumpkin seed?"

"They say once you've tasted the water of the Punkinseed you'll always come back."

"I certainly intend to see it one more time whether I taste it or not. On my way back to civilization. And the sooner the better." She dabbed perspiration and dust off her forehead with a silk hanky, surprised at her boldness.

"Camp Clarke is down yonder. We cross a bridge there."

"A town? Do they have a hotel?" Perhaps she could stay there until Franklin came for her!

"For a dollar Mr. Clarke will let you sleep on the floor of the post office."

At Camp Clarke a man wearing a derby hat slouched by the bridge. He barely moved. "That'll be two and a half dollars for the rig and one dollar for your passenger. And Mr. Clarke don't take no greenbacks."

From a saddle bag under the seat the red-bearded man pulled a small leather pouch. He took off his gloves and fumbled in the pouch. Finally with some irritation he said, "Ma'am, will you get a dollar and a quarter eagle out of my poke?"

Silently she took the pouch. She saw how huge his hands were. She felt their great strength. For some reason that both pleased her and made her angry. She moved away from him. Her deft fingers sifted through coins in the pouch.

"Here, sir." She handed two tiny gold coins to the man with the derby.

"All right. Go slow," growled the man. The boards of the bridge creaked and groaned as the wagon rumbled onto the bridge. The man yelled, "Mr. Clarke may have to start charging you extry. You're going to bust our bridge someday. What are carrying, Jonah? Cannon balls?"

Jonah! That was his name. The team plodded very slowly across the bridge. Holly remained as far away from red-bearded Jonah as she could. She plunged her thoughts into the surging current. Rivers always seemed never-ending and profound and purposeful to Holly. They were so obviously God's creation. She felt herself calmed.

Jonah's voice surprised her. "Care for some dodgers and jerky?" He held open a bag of buckskin.

"No, thank you. I have food in my basket." She was sick of sausage, pickles, hard-boiled eggs, and hard bread. But who knew if a cactus was ground up in these dodgers? Who knew if this jerky was dried rattlesnake?

He cleared his throat. "Back there in Sidney, uhhh…" He scuffed the floorboard of the wagon with his boot. He looked for all the world like a horse pawing the ground. It was so boyish she wanted to put him at ease. But her tongue was frozen. She didn't know why. She had always been that way, knowing what to say, yet not being able to say anything personal. Even with girls her own age. It made her angry to be so shy.

"Yes?" she asked angrily.

He almost whispered, "I said somebody said something about you being as thin as a stick. I'm sorry if I hurt your feelings."

"Thin as a stick?" And he had to say it a second time! "I would have to respect your opinion for it to hurt my feelings. And I don't."

"I kind of shot it back because you snapped at me."

"I do not snap!"

"It's not true anyway. You're not that thin—"

"Oh, thank you," she sputtered sarcastically.

"You're a pleasure to look at. Really. Your skin is as fresh and clear and soft I'll bet as a baby's." His mouth fell open and eyes widened as if he were discovering all this for the first time. "And your eyes are alive and innocent as a deer's."

"How poetic." Holly turned her back on him. She was angry with herself. She was embarrassed that she didn't know how to handle a compliment. Deep inside, she was pleased by what he had said. It was crude as mud but wonderful. Why couldn't a respectable man have ever said that to her in real poetry? Why did the first compliments in her life from a man other than Papa have to come from a frontier roughneck with a face hidden behind a red bush? He was probably lying anyway. She wasn't going to ever become a silly flirty goose like some of the young ladies she knew at Gladwyne School. She would be more like Mrs. Snade. But she didn't want to be like Mrs. Snade. She wasn't ever going to think of Mrs. Snade again. She really felt like crying. It had been such an awful day. And it wasn't getting any better.

The afternoon became drier and hotter. The ride was much bumpier too on the prairie north of the Platte River. When the same mail rider blasted past them, this time going north to Camp Robinson and riding a different sweat-lathered horse, he was far away from them. He didn't wave.

Holly said, "I should have given him a note for Franklin, so he would know I was coming."

"Franklin already knows," Jonah replied. "The station master telegraphed him."

"Why is the mail rider so far away from us?"

"He's riding the main trail."

"And we're not?"

"Best not to be, ma'am."

Holly shuddered. And she worried. The sun was sinking into the vast grassy plain to the west. Would they not make it to the station before nightfall? She was terrified to be in the wilderness at night. But she was even more terrified by being alone, unprotected with this strange man. What might he try?

She broke a long silence. "Aren't we close to that station yet?"

"Not close enough." His voice was worried.

"What do you mean by that?" Then she saw dust ahead. Men were approaching on horses. "Indians?" She began shaking. "Wh...wh...where is your six-shooter?"

"I don't carry one."

three

Three men thundered right up to the wagon before reining in their horses, billowing rude dust over the wagon. All three were bearded under black, floppy wide-brimmed hats. Holly had never seen such filthy men before. She felt ill.

"Where've you been, Finch?" demanded one bearded man. The filth was even in his voice. "We had business this morning. Did you forget?"

"No. The shipment was a day late," answered Jonah easily. "And besides, I'm doing a favor for Lieutenant Bennington."

"Oh. I get it." The man tried to smile. "That's good of you to help the nice lieutenant." For the first time he acknowledged Holly. "Who's under that fancy umbreller? Is that the lieutenant's little filly, is it?"

"She happens to be his sister," said Jonah.

"She'd be available then?" And the man rode closer and gave Holly a hungry-eyed look that she never wanted to see again. It made her shudder.

Oh, God, she prayed, *please let us go.*

"We have to go." Jonah flicked the reins.

One of the men snickered, "Don't forget where to leave the goods, Finch."

The bearded man who seemed to be the leader snapped, "Shut up, you fool!"

The three men turned and rode north. Holly almost said "friends of yours?" in her driest, most disapproving voice, but suddenly she realized the men were friends of his and she didn't want to know anything more about Jonah Finch.

In the low rays of the sun, the station was a welcome sight. It was no more than a flat-roofed sod cabin. Nearby was a much larger lean-to, inside a sprawling corral full of horses and mules. Jonah drove the wagon to the corral gate, jumped down, and hurriedly began unhitching the four mules.

"Howdy, ma'am."

The voice surprised Holly. She looked down to see a hatless, white-bearded man extending his arms up toward her. His face was a map of creases.

"How do you do, sir," she said stiffly.

"Get yourself down here and we'll get you inside out of this sun."

"Thank you," she murmured.

"By golly, your dress is dusty enough to plow."

The sod cabin was surprisingly cool inside. It even seemed clean. The dirt floor was packed down hard as rock. No dust rose from the man's shuffling boots. Across one end of the cabin hung a dark curtain.

"I'm Nehemiah Campbell, ma'am. Just an old stock tender for this station. But I ain't never done nothing I had to apologize to the good Lord for."

"Unlike Jonah Finch?"

"Oh, for sure I ain't like Jonah." The man scratched his head. "So you seen Jonah is a strange feller too, did you? You might be right about him. He ain't straight for some reason, but I can't figure out why."

"Why would you tell all that to me, a perfect stranger?" Holly felt very bold with the older man. If only she could be that way with every one.

"I don't hardly think of you as a stranger. I been expecting you for days. Your brother was here just a few days ago, asking me a hundred questions. You worried him pretty good, not showing up when he thought you would."

"Then why didn't he meet me in Sidney himself?"

"The army must have had other plans for him." Nehemiah winked slyly and whispered, "I hear tell he's sniffing out gunrunners."

"Gunrunners!"

Nehemiah whispered, "There's a fortune in it. Any Sioux warrior will trade his whole poke of Black Hills gold for a repeating rifle." He stopped and listened. Holly heard noise outside, too. Nehemiah winked, then boomed, "There's a wash basin behind that curtain. Rest your bones a while on that bed back there. I just put a clean blanket on it. I'll tell you when we got some grub fixed."

Behind the curtain Holly brushed off her clothes, washed the dust from her face and hands, then warily poked the bed. A few days ago she would have been appalled by the bed, which was no more than a rickety bench with a worn blanket thrown over it. The trail had lowered her standards even more than the railroad had.

Then she realized how helpless she was. Would it be safe to lie down so close to two complete strangers? She remembered the filthy men on the trail. They were friends of Jonah. What if they came back? But she was so tired. She had to rest on the blanket. She lay on her side, curled in a ball, and stared at the closed curtain. Fear crawled on her like a snake. But she was so tired...

When Holly woke up, it took her a long worrisome time to remember where she was. This was not Gladwyne. This was not the Betsy Ross Hotel. The train? No. She fought the feeling of dread in her stomach. Then she remembered. She got up stiffly. Where were the two strange men? How could she protect herself through the long dangerous night? She opened the shutters of a window. There was no glass in it. The sun burned low on the horizon. The air was delicious. Did the prairie cool off so rapidly in the evening?

Then she realized she was looking east!

She heard Nehemiah's crusty voice beyond the curtain, "She's a purty one all right. Bright-eyed as a calf. Light as a feather too."

"A might frail," mumbled a deeper voice.

"You young buck, listen to the wise words of an old man who grew up with eight sisters. That little gal is a late bloomer. I can tell. Four or five years from now she'll be the fairest rose between Sidney and Deadwood. Men will be busting each other up over her."

"Ahhh." But the deeper voice sounded pleased.

Holly was thrilled. Could Nehemiah be right? Or was he just a frontier leg-twister? Did he think she was listening? But she did remember her mama was pretty and all rounded. She quickly freshened herself in the wash basin and pulled back the curtain. Jonah and Nehemiah were eating at a table.

"What happened?" she asked. "Did I sleep through the entire night?"

Nehemiah laughed. "By George, I never did see such a tired critter in my whole life."

"Critter!" she cried.

"Sorry, ma'am," chuckled Nehemiah. "But you sure were sleeping hard. I tried to wake you up for some real good grub—salt pork and navy beans and corn bread—but you wouldn't stir. So I figured you must have needed that sleep powerful bad."

"You didn't want us to shake you awake, did you, ma'am?" asked Jonah, not so innocently.

"Certainly not," huffed Holly. But she was surprised at his appearance. His hair and beard seemed more auburn than red.

"Sit down here and eat, ma'am." Jonah stood up and offered her his chair. "I'm going out to hitch up the mules." She was startled. She actually saw his eyes appraising her for the first time. They weren't hidden inside a squint under the dark shadow of his hat brim. They were deep blue and pleased with her.

"Corn cakes and molasses, ma'am," announced Nehemiah proudly.

"Fine," answered Holly absentmindedly. Why couldn't she get her mind off that red-bearded roughneck?

"Sorry I can't offer you quail eggs. They're small but real tasty. But, shucks, I couldn't find any this morning."

"That's quite all right," Holly said with complete sincerity. "Perhaps someday you could keep chickens here."

"I had some. But the wolves got them."

"Wolves?"

Nehemiah left the cabin. A few minutes later he returned. "I cook outside in the summer, ma'am. Got to keep my little bungalow nice and cool like."

On the tin plate were three crusty pancakes made of cornmeal. She had never eaten such crude fare in her life. But she suspected Nehemiah made them special for her. So she acted enthusiastic as she poured thick molasses on one.

Nehemiah puttered around the room, talking constantly. "Glad to see you without all that prairie on your face and a real purty face it is."

"Thank you." She didn't have to pretend to be pleased. She didn't have to pretend to be pleased with the corn cakes either. She was very hungry and they weren't sausage or pickles or hard-boiled eggs or hard bread. Besides all that, they tasted good. She even drank two cups of Nehemiah's muddy coffee.

"Now you just keep eating like that, ma'am. You got to keep adding kindling for the fire. By golly, I see color's blazing in your cheeks already. You'll make it out here. You just need to get some padding on that little frame of yours. Why when I lifted you off the wagon yesterday I thought to myself, 'She don't weigh no more than a hundred pound sack of corn meal.' But I was telling Jonah that little gal is going to be a late bloomer…"

Holly half-listened to Nehemiah. He never seemed to stop talking. She must have looked like a walking statue of dust the day before. But she couldn't worry about it now. She faced another hot dry dusty day in the same bone-rattling freight wagon.

"Thank you for your hospitality, Mr. Campbell."

"Ain't nothing. I'm sorry to see you leave. I won't see another face as purty as yours for ten years. And I've seen a gob of faces on the stagecoach when it stops here to change the horses."

"What stagecoach?"

"The one that runs between Sidney and Deadwood."

"Does it go to Camp Robinson?"

"It surely does, ma'am."

"Why didn't I get to ride the stagecoach?"

"Because it ain't made a run for two weeks. Not since it got robbed by Fly Speck Billy and his toughs. Some folks say Dirty Doak did it. Don't believe it, ma'am. He's too busy smuggling whisky to the soldiers."

"If the stagecoach ever runs again, you can expect to see my face one last time. I intend to go back east."

"That'd be a real shame, ma'am. We need ladies like you out here on the frontier. You just don't know how much. You're the glue for the best makings we Americans have to offer. By George, I was telling a feller just the other day..."

Nehemiah was still talking to her as the wagon rumbled away. When Nehemiah's voice could no longer be heard, Jonah chuckled. "Folks hereabouts call him Blabby. He never had a thought he didn't pass on to the rest of the world."

"Did you ever hear him tell a lie?"

Jonah raised an eyebrow. "No, I haven't."

So there was something crooked about Jonah. Nehemiah said so. Holly glanced back. She could no longer see Nehemiah's station. How had Blabby lived so long being honest around such treacherous cutthroats?

The day and prairie seemed endless. Down on the main trail the mail rider had thundered past going south, lunch was long over, and Jonah had whistled a dozen tunes by the time Holly saw something peculiar about the green plain of grass that stretched north ahead of them. The plain stopped abruptly against yellow bluffs. The afternoon sky seemed filled with white streamers. Holly was surprised to see careful rectangular patterns on the plain.

"Camp Robinson!" she cried.

"Yes, ma'am."

She sputtered, "You might have told me." But she couldn't be angry. She was too happy. And in spite of herself she felt strangely attracted to this man. But surely it was just gratitude for getting her safely to Franklin.

She strained her eyes. Long, low barracks buildings laid out in several rectangles covered a large area. There was no wall around the camp. That was why it was not called a fort. That was a good sign, she thought.

To the east and farther north toward the bluffs were thousands of tan triangles.

Tepees!

Smoke rose from the midst of the tepees in hundreds of places. Her heart was beating fast, stampeded by fear! She seemed transported to another planet. The panorama had suddenly become so overwhelmingly alien. She had never felt so out of place.

She realized dogs were barking. They never stopped. Beyond the tepees on the plain were dark masses. Seeming to move but not move. Horses? But there must have been many thousands of horses!

She began to hear other sounds: babies crying, children screaming in delight, horses whinnying, wagons rattling. Blue-uniformed white men scurried about on foot, on horseback, and in wagons. Log buildings seemed everywhere. How puny had been her images of the camp and the reservation!

Almost all the soldiers waved and smiled.

When Jonah finally stopped in front of one of six mud-brick cottages, Holly was still stunned by the strangeness. But when she saw a blue-uniformed man walk out from under the porch of the cottage her heart soared.

Seconds later she threw herself down into his waiting arms.

"Oh, Franklin!"

He hugged her. "Here at last, little Holly."

She noticed a woman there too. Holly pulled back, slightly embarrassed. "Little?"

Franklin took the arm of the woman. "Holly, this is Esmeralda Monroe, my very good friend."

"Hello, Holly," said Esmeralda. She smiled politely with closed lips. Her blonde hair was pulled severely back and bunned. But Holly had to admit most men would think Esmeralda's olive-skinned "Mona Lisa" look beautiful, if a trifle square-jawed. And then she noticed her green eyes sparkled like emeralds!

"It's so nice to meet you, Miss Monroe," Holly said with some enthusiasm after realizing the gray of Esmeralda's organdy dress was far too dull and dark for a proper young lady. But who would care in this wilderness? Perhaps even Franklin didn't notice.

As Jonah walked around the wagon, Esmeralda's full lips spread in delight. Her teeth were pearls. "Jonah Finch! How was the trip?"

"Fine, ma'am." And he hefted two of Holly's bags off the wagon.

"Wait!" cried Franklin. "I can take care of her bags. You shouldn't—" He suddenly stopped as Jonah seemed to give him the slightest scowl. What was going on? Holly watched them closely. Nothing more was exchanged between the two men as Jonah lugged bags and cardboard boxes into the cottage.

Franklin said, "Esmeralda's father is the post commander, Colonel Monroe."

"How nice," said Holly. As usual she was at a loss for words, even though a thousand thoughts thrashed though her head. If only Papa had sent her to finishing school sooner. She smiled lamely.

Esmeralda rescued her. "How can Holly even think? I remember that trip up here from Sidney. The dust sifts right inside your brain. You must be exhausted, my dear." Esmeralda took her arm and squeezed her hand.

Franklin and Esmeralda chatted, so merrily and so obviously comforting Holly that she became even angrier at herself for once again being an empty vessel socially. She noticed through her cloud of frustration that the cottage had one front door. Franklin must have the entire cottage. She eyed uncomprehendingly the ribbons and insignias on his dark blue uniform.

Jonah finally joined them. He tipped his hat and smiled. "Mission accomplished. I hereby resign from this here United States Army."

"Franklin, you must have a million things to say to Holly and she's very tired besides," gushed Esmeralda. "I really must get back home. Jonah will escort me."

"Of course," agreed Jonah. But he sounded nervous.

"Good-bye." Franklin had some pain in his eyes as Esmeralda left arm in arm with Jonah.

Holly watched them, too. She sighed. "If only he would shave off that horrible bush. I can't tell if he's twenty or forty."

"A shade under thirty I would guess."

Esmeralda and Jonah turned up a walk toward a large house. Holly saw his easy youthful swagger. She remembered the strength in his hands. She found herself wishing he was more than just a roughneck. "Just what does Mr. Finch do?" she asked.

"He does odd jobs. He'll scout for the army or run an errand or two. A lot of civilians like to hang around camps and forts. They survive by doing a little of this and doing a little of that."

"Everyone on the trail seems to know him."

"He gets around."

"Some of them seemed...evil."

"Don't rely too much on first impressions out here. Some pretty seedy-looking men are all right. They didn't have our advantages, Holly."

"Your advantages—"

Franklin smiled. "Say! Rest up and I'll take you into the reservation. You can meet the famous—"

"Stop! I must say something first. I want to go back east. I mean after we visit a day or two of course. I don't want to stay here. I'm a fish out of water here."

"Of course you can go anywhere you like," Franklin smiled and waved her through the open door, "if first you find a position I approve of. I am your guardian until you are twenty-one you know."

"I can find work. Just give me enough money to go back and meet expenses until I find work."

"Far too risky, dear sister."

"Risky!" She felt her face redden. She had forgotten how difficult Franklin could be. After all, she hadn't seen him more than a few minutes at a time since Mama died. She had been eleven and Franklin seventeen. Eight years ago! That sad thought cooled her anger. Confronting Franklin wouldn't work. She must think of other strategies. She could blubber pitifully and throw herself on the floor. No, that would not work. He would be even less likely to trust her by herself. But there was a way.

"Why are you so pensive, little sister?"

She smiled. "It might not be so bad here. I guess I was over-reacting from riding a bucking freight wagon for two days."

"I'll fix tea." Franklin seemed distracted. He kept glancing out the front window.

"Do you have time?"

"Just a minute!" He opened the front door. He yelled, "Get away from that wagon, soldier!" He closed the door and smiled. His eyes widened at her seventeen bags and eleven cardboard boxes stacked in an adjacent room. "Is all that yours? Where are all Mama's nice Saratoga trunks?"

"Auctioned off, I suppose," she snapped accusingly. But she

had no time to indulge her resentment. She quickly added, "Don't you have duties around the camp? After all, you were too busy to come to Sidney to get me." She just couldn't keep the sting out of her comments.

Franklin took a deep breath as if to bolster his patience. "I didn't know when you would arrive. Besides, there was a little fuss here at the reservation."

"With the Sioux Indians?"

"Sioux is a French word. They call themselves Lakota." Franklin kept glancing out the window. His voice wandered, too. "But they are contrary. Even though they don't like the word 'Sioux' they don't want us to use their word 'Lakota.' It somehow soils it."

"I think I understand." It was all Holly could do to keep from laughing, because being contrary was exactly how she herself was going to behave. She intended to become the most contrary, exasperating person Franklin had ever met. He would be glad to send her east.

But that wasn't even the best part of her plan. She could hardly wait for Franklin to go out for a while. "Are you sure you don't have some duties?"

He frowned out the window. "There is something I need to do. I won't be gone long." He hurried outside.

Holly laughed.

Now she would really light the fire and get her plan simmering.

four

"Good-bye, Franklin." Holly giggled nervously as she peeked out the window to make sure he was really going to leave her alone. She was surprised to see him climb into Jonah's wagon and flick the reins. Why would Franklin bother with Jonah's old freight wagon? Maybe he was embarrassed to have it sitting in front of his cottage. The wagon lurched away.

"I have no time to mull over such a tiny mystery."

She glanced around the living room, seeing it for the first time. One stuffed sofa and two stuffed chairs faced a lifeless fireplace. A hallway led to the back of the cottage. But she had no time to explore. A door led into a large room with nothing in it but her luggage and a bookcase and a small desk by the front window.

She quickly opened the top desk drawer. Yes, Franklin had some very nice quill pens and she could make do with his black ink. But his stationery was much too plain for her task. She located the cardboard box that held her packet of stationery. From the packet she selected stationery bordered in flowers—her favorite, white magnolias. The crisp sheets of paper even smelled of magnolias.

She sat down at the desk. She felt like she had felt after acting like Miss Snade with the conductor on the Pennsylvania Railroad. She felt hot and cool, happy and sad, enthused and depressed. This was no small decision. This was the biggest decision of her life she suddenly realized. Oh, why hadn't she done it quickly? Why did she have to think so much?

What she was about to do was dishonest. But it was the only way she could think of to rescue herself from a life of misery. So surely God thought it was all right for her to do it. She couldn't think of a verse from the Bible that confirmed her opinion exactly. And she certainly didn't have to time to look for one. She had to act quickly—before Franklin got back.

She should say a quick prayer for God to forgive her. But she really didn't have time to do that either. Franklin might return any second, and her plan was much too important to delay.

In the upper right hand corner she hastily wrote:

June 10, 1877
c/o Lieutenant Franklin Bennington
Camp Robinson, Nebraska

She deliberated over how to greet Granville Wiggins III. Should she sound formal? *Dear Mr. Wiggins,* she thought. No. This was no time for that aloofness. *My dear Mr. Wiggins,* she wondered. That was closest to her intent. He could be a dear, she supposed. But it was still too distant. He might not feel her warmth. *Dearest Mr. Wiggins.* She quickly dismissed that as too self-contradictory. She reflected on the last two days, clenched her teeth and wrote:

My dearest Granville:
I so enjoyed our last visit. You were the
perfect host. No one realizes more than I how my
unannounced arrival interfered with your
wonderfully busy schedule. But you dropped all
your pressing business, like the true gentleman
you are, and gave me such comfort.
I know you will be interested the details of my
trip into the savage wilderness. You are inter-
ested in all things about you—a true Renais-
sance man.
Words cannot express my horror of the reality
of this place. In all candor, Franklin has slipped
below the level of civility. He entrusted my

*delivery to a fiery-haired barbarian named
Jonah Finch, whom everyone on the trail hails
as if he is none other than Jesse James himself.
What the roughneck does for a living is a
mystery to all but the lowest forms of humanity.*

    *All crimes seem in vogue here. Immensely
profitable is smuggling whisky to the soldiers,
but most profitable of all is smuggling guns to
the Indians. Apparently the Indians have hoards
of Black Hills gold—nuggets no doubt—they will
gladly trade in bucketsful for a repeating rifle,
whatever that is.*

    *So you see my predicament: I am a fragile
rose among wilderness cacti and rampaging
hogs.*

    *Only you can help me, my dearest Granville. I
will require of you only a short letter offering me
employment as a governess or a teacher or a
clerk or whatever sounds respectable. Naturally
you will be stretching the truth. But it is no more
than a stretch. After your letter reassures
Franklin that I have employment, I will be able
to leave this devastation and return to Philadelphia. I will find employment there I'm sure.*

Holly paused and reread her letter to Granville. It was a mas-
terpiece. Of that she was certain. She added one sentence:
"Please send the letter to me as soon as possible."

Now how should she end it? *Sincerely yours?* Too stiff. *Sincerely?* Still too stiff. *Your friend?* Too childish. Finally she
settled on *Most cordially yours, Holly B.*

The *B* was a nice touch. Now how was she to mail it? She
wanted to mail it immediately—in minutes, in seconds. But
where were stamps? And where was the post office?

As she sat immobile, her scheme made her queasy. And the

queasy feeling didn't disappear even as she reread her letter to Granville about bad men and rifles and Indians and such scary things. But what choice did she have? When she heard someone clomp onto the front porch of the cottage she quickly sealed the letter and returned to the living room.

Franklin entered. "Rested up any?"

"Oh yes, I feel better." She had to tell a lie. Or were there two lies? Well, who could blame her? She had tried to tell Franklin about how crooked Jonah Finch was and Franklin had just brushed her off. And wasn't it Franklin who entrusted her care to a wild, unpredictable roughneck like Jonah? Hadn't Franklin forced her to come to this wilderness? Hadn't he done what was expedient for himself? Why shouldn't she shade the truth a little? Her situation was desperate.

"You're holding a letter."

"I wrote it last night at the station." How many lies was that now? They seemed to come forth with every breath. "May we go out and post this?"

"Of course. If you're rested I'll show you around some. I'll get a buggy."

She relaxed until he returned.

With no ceremony Franklin walked her to a covered buggy, new and shiny black with soft leather seats. It was hitched to a spirited white horse. Franklin was so nonchalant about such a wonderful rig Holly knew he must have used it frequently, probably for the square-jawed Esmeralda.

Esmeralda was an important part of Holly's overall strategy. And, as if that part had to be initiated with no delay, Franklin headed the buggy west and pointed to the large house Esmeralda entered. "That is the house of the post commander."

Holly hesitated. Could she carry out her plan? She glanced around at the threatening, wide open spaces. Where were the cozy two-story houses and lamp posts and bricked streets? Who could blame her for what she had to do?

"Did you hear me, Holly, dear?" asked Franklin. "That's the

house of the post commander, Colonel Monroe."

"And his spinster daughter."

"You made a quick judgment!" he said, not angry because he wasn't sure if Holly was joking.

"She's not right for you." Holly felt very sick. She wasn't lying. She really meant it. But she felt sick anyway.

Franklin's face was pink. "She's coming out now. Please don't say anything unpleasant."

Esmeralda stepped off the front porch. She smiled sweetly. Holly had not noticed her dimples before. "Won't you come in and have some refreshments?" asked Esmeralda in a light, sweet voice.

"I have to mail a letter," answered Holly rudely.

"Thank you for the invitation," added Franklin quickly. "But I'm showing Holly the camp. Even though she is extremely tired, I now realize." He looked at Holly sympathetically. "Why don't you join us, Esmeralda?"

"Isn't the buggy rather small?" asked Holly. She stared at Esmeralda as if she weighed at least three hundred pounds, instead of little more than one hundred. Holly could feel Franklin's anger beside her.

"You need time with your sister," answered Esmeralda politely. She held her hands together in a prayerful way. She was really getting on Holly's nerves. But Holly must not show her anger. A breezy cheerfulness was part of Holly's deceit. After all, wasn't Esmeralda doing the very same thing to her?

"Perhaps you can get together with that Jonah Finch," said Holly innocently. "Or is he still inside?"

"No. He left some time ago." Esmeralda was still smiling. She was not going to be as easy to rile as Franklin.

"We really must be going," said Franklin.

"Franklin, why be in such a hurry?" pleaded Holly. "Can't you see Esperanza has nothing to do."

"I wouldn't say that." Esmeralda was finally showing pink at the base of her throat. Her hands had fallen apart.

"Would you welcome the company of Jonah Finch?" asked Holly.

"I welcome most visitors," said Esmeralda softly. Her hands balled into fists.

"We have to go," said Franklin abruptly.

"If I see Jonah Finch I'll tell him you would welcome his company, Esperanza." called Holly as the buggy bounced west.

After a minute Franklin reined the horse to a stop. "What in the world were you doing back there?" he asked angrily.

"She isn't right for you, Franklin. Thank God I got here in time to stop you from doing something disastrous. Let me assess the local belles for you, so you don't make a terrible mistake. Esperanza is wearing a dress a matron would have worn to a ball five years ago."

"Listen to me, little sister," hissed Franklin. "Her name is Esmeralda. And it's very difficult for ladies on the frontier to have the latest fashions. And most of all, you are not to interfere in my life."

"You seemed to have no compunction about interfering with mine, uprooting me from civilization."

"I'm your guardian!" he sputtered.

"You didn't let me finish. I mistakenly thought it was interference. I mistakenly thought this was the wilderness. But now that I'm here, I'm glad." How many lies did she just rattle off? Three?

"You are glad?" Franklin eyed his sister doubtfully.

She just smiled sweetly, like Esmeralda.

Franklin pointed west, beyond the post commander's house, to a large building. He said grumpily, "That's the post trader's building."

Holly shuddered. "Do the Sioux buy things there?"

"No. They have their own trader. This one is for soldiers and civilians."

"Like Jonah Finch."

"Yes."

"Does the trader sell whisky?"

"Yes. But no one is allowed more than two drinks in one day."

"I imagine Jonah would approve of that."

"I didn't know you thought so highly of him."

"I don't. He probably smuggles whisky to the soldiers and he can get a much better price if whisky is rationed here at the camp."

"Let's move on." Franklin didn't deny Jonah was a whisky-runner. He turned the buggy south. He nodded at a building. "That's the hospital."

Franklin cooled off as he rattled on about buildings for the physician, the wheelwright, the prisoners, the bakers, the butchers, the carpenters, the laundresses, and on and on. Holly stopped listening. As they rode south in the buggy, Holly tried to estimate how long it would take to receive Granville Wiggins III's reply to her masterful plea. One day to Sidney. Three days to Philadelphia. Two days with Granville Wiggins III. Three days back to Sidney. One day to Camp Robinson.

"Ten days," she mumbled.

"What was that?" asked Franklin, finally in a good mood again.

"Nothing," she lied. Ten days. Two weeks at the most. That would be her minimum sentence in this desolate wilderness.

Satisfied with her calculations, she assessed Franklin. He was tan and clean shaven. He too had a wide forehead and a slightly concave nose. He looked more like a choir boy than an officer. He certainly didn't look like a warrior. His almost blond hair was lighter than hers and looked very fine against his blue forage cap. The cap displayed crossed brass sabers. Above the sabers was a brass 3. Below was the letter A in brass. He wore a dark blue jacket belted at the waist. On each shoulder was a yellow fabric bar. Down the outside of each leg of his sky blue pants ran a broad yellow stripe. High black riding boots gleamed like mirrors. He held the reins with black gauntlets.

As far as Holly could see, Franklin was completely unarmed. How dangerous could the camp be if he went about unarmed?

"There are the barracks for the enlisted foot soldiers," he said, frowning. "Nothing interesting there."

Holly scoured the barracks. Franklin was such an inept liar. "Oh look, there's Jonah," she blurted. Her heart skipped. What a peculiar effect the roughneck Jonah had on her. But surely she was just thinking of carrying out her scheme. "Let's talk to him," she suggested.

"Why? I thought you didn't like him."

"I'm open-minded. Please stop."

"Be careful what you say, please." His voice was tinged with distrust.

That should have pleased her. After all, Franklin's dismay with her bizarre behavior was part of her plan. But she felt sick instead. She told herself her queasiness was just a fragment of her enormous submerged unhappiness about coming west bobbing to the surface. It had nothing to do with her plan.

The buggy rolled to a stop not ten feet from Jonah, who was shirtless and bending over a wash basin in back of the barracks. He had not seen the buggy. He was splashing water in his face. Muscles rippled in his broad back. His beard was dripping soap. He held out his hands and groped the air.

A small girl beside him handed him a towel and eyed the buggy suspiciously. The girl was about four or five. She absentmindedly stroked two black braided pigtails. Her dress was brightly beaded buckskin with a fringe on the bottom. Her face was sunny and coppery.

Holly called, "Mr. Finch!"

Jonah Finch turned, still dabbing his face with the towel, and seemed unsurprised. "Why, it's the Benningtons."

"Who is your friend?" asked Holly cheerfully.

Jonah laughed. "Why, this is Red Wing, the niece of Running Lark, the wife of the post trader Louie Boudreau. Red Wing and I are very old friends."

Red Wing's face was stony now. She resented Holly's attention. Suddenly she ran toward the trading post. Holly wanted to cry, Don't go! but she really did need the undivided attention of Jonah and Franklin. She would make it up to Red Wing another time.

She said, "Did you get your wagon unloaded, Mr. Finch?"

Jonah gave Franklin a peculiar look. "Yes, ma'am."

"Good. We wouldn't want all the profits to go to Dirty Doak."

Franklin gasped. "Holly, what are you saying?"

Holly ignored him. "Why don't you shave off that beard, Mr. Finch? I'm sure Esmeralda would appreciate it." Holly could feel Franklin's hot glare. Her plan was really cooking now.

"And would you appreciate it too, ma'am?" Jonah stood barechested, with his hands on his hips.

Holly flushed. Jonah Finch was blatantly defiant. How dare he turn things around on her! The impertinence! "Your bushy disguise is no affair of mine, Mr. Finch."

"You're the only one who had made that request," he said casually. "I thought your interest was personal."

She had shown anger instead of a breezy cheerfulness. How had her plan become so botched? "I only mentioned it, sir, so you could court Esmeralda like a proper gentleman. For heaven's sakes, put your shirt on!"

Franklin grunted, "Sorry but we have to go post a letter, Jonah." He flicked the reins and the buggy lurched away.

Holly's aggravation with Jonah Finch quickly vanished. Mailing the letter was an essential part of her scheme. She had been very smart to have such a many-pronged strategy. No matter what Franklin did, his every action seemed to advance one of her plans to get out the wilderness with no unnecessary delay.

"There's the adjutant's office," grumbled Franklin. "Give me the letter." She had never seen him so sulky.

She handed him the letter. "Please make sure they know

where Pennsylvania is before you surrender my letter."

He rolled his eyes, probably resisting a sarcastic remark, then frowned at the envelope. "Who is this Granville Wiggins III?"

"A gentleman who called on me at the Gladwyne School."

Franklin's face softened. "How dense of me. You have a beau."

"Yes." She felt genuinely sad.

"I should have known. I was seeing you with the eyes of an older brother." He stared at her. "You are grown up." He quickly added, "Almost." He shook his head. "You're going to be quite a belle."

Franklin's unexpected compliment pleased Holly. How could she make him miserable after he had said such wonderful things about her? She would have plenty of opportunities to carry out her aggravation. But no, she mustn't weaken. She would never get out of the wilderness if she got softhearted.

"Please make sure it goes east by the fastest possible means," she snapped.

Franklin sighed and went inside to post her letter with the adjutant. After he returned he guided the buggy around the eastern flank of the post. They passed more long barracks for both foot soldiers and cavalry.

Holly asked dryly, "How long do these men serve?"

"Five years."

"Five years! No wonder Esperanza looks good."

Farther east lay a vast field of tan tepees with dozens of unseen fires streaming gray smoke up into the sky. Holly's cutting remarks died in her throat. She was terrified of Indians.

When they finally returned to the cottage Holly was shocked to see who was waiting.

five

"Jonah." She quickly corrected herself, "I meant Mr. Finch. You've shaved your beard!"

Jonah made an exaggerated bow. "I honored your request, Miss Bennington."

He had indeed shaved his dark red beard. His face was startlingly white where the beard had been. She felt shameless the way she drank in his exposed face. He had wide thin lips over a strong chin. His nose was long and straight, no longer dwarfed by his bushy beard. She had already seen the pleasure in his penetrating blue eyes.

"Come and sit on the porch with us, Jonah," said Franklin.

"Yes—I mean no," said Holly. "Mr. Finch is on his way to see Esmeralda, I'm sure."

"If you say so." Jonah laughed.

"Jonah, won't you please stay with Holly while I put the buggy away?" asked Franklin, still visibly angry over her many remarks. "Then I have to assemble at retreat."

And in a flash Franklin had gone away in the buggy.

"What was he talking about?" Holly asked in confusion.

"All the soldiers at the camp assemble in the parade ground at sunset. It's called retreat. The sergeant of Company A will take roll and report the results to Franklin. The sergeants of all the companies in the camp do that for their lieutenant or captain."

Holly noticed that blue-uniformed soldiers were gathering in the open space south of the cottage. They were on foot. Their trousers had white stripes. But didn't Franklin's pants have yellow stripes?

She didn't have time to ponder such tiny mysteries. It was a wonderful opportunity for Holly to expound to Jonah Finch on the virtues of Esmeralda. Or was it? Didn't she want Franklin to hear her encouragement too? How could Franklin become exasperated beyond measure if he wasn't there to hear her? She would wait until Franklin returned. She found herself very pleased with that decision.

"You are smiling, Miss Bennington. Does my appearance please you?"

"How can you think such a thing? I've never met anyone as impudent as you, sir."

"Please have a seat." He waved to a group of wicker chairs on the porch. "It is customary here for folks to sit on the porch and talk."

"And become the source of gossip?"

"No one will gossip, unless we remain standing. Then they will suspect something highly charged."

She remained standing on the porch. Jonah was on the walk. Their eyes were level. She found herself wishing he would look at her—look into her eyes. She felt very bold. Perhaps it was because she had a role to play. She was the cupid who would push Jonah and Esmeralda together. It certainly couldn't be for any other reason. Even if he was far better looking than she imagined. But he was still just a roughneck drifter or something worse.

He grinned. "I'm flattered. You do wish us to be the subject of gossip."

What was she thinking? That wasn't part of her plan. "Of course not," she huffed and sat down in a wicker chair.

He sat down on the bottom step and leaned back on his elbow. It must have been his way of being respectful. He took off his wide-brimmed tan hat. His hair was cut short and brushed back. The sinking rays of the sun made it glow reddish blonde. His hair was becoming a source of amazement for her. At times it was blond, at times red, at times auburn. It seemed almost brown sometimes, too. Was Jonah himself as many faceted?

She could easily believe so. She was glad he wasn't looking at her. She could study him. She found herself wishing she could touch his hair. Was it soft?

She heard the piercing blast of an urgent bugle.

The parade ground was choked with men and horses! Soldiers stood in long rows. And behind them were rows of mounted soldiers. Where was Franklin? There were so many soldiers. She watched as what she supposed were orders and replies to orders were barked back and forth. The American flag was lowered on a tall flag pole. Soon the entire assembly broke apart. The sun had dipped out of sight, but the gray night sky still seemed full of order and safety. And strangely, Jonah Finch belonged. She found she wanted to hold the moment.

"You two are sure quiet." It was Franklin. He had returned. "But that was a great sunset tonight."

Franklin sat down in a wicker chair next to Holly. He appeared in good spirits again. She could tell he was anxious about something though. His fingers tapped the arm of the chair.

Holly would give him reason to be anxious. "I'm sure Esmeralda will be so pleased to see you cared enough for her to actually shave off your beard, Mr. Finch."

"Are you pleased, Holly?" asked Franklin.

"Franklin!" she snapped. What was he doing? Didn't he remember how sensitive she was about men?

Franklin smiled. "It looks good, Jonah. I'm sure Holly will agree after more reflection. After all, she recommended it."

"So I did," she mumbled glumly.

She could think of nothing more to say. She knew the two men were speaking, but she couldn't follow their conversation. Their words seemed as elusive as butterflies, while a million thoughts flickered through her brain like dusty moths around a lantern. Were Franklin and Jonah involved in something together? What had she started? Was Jonah interested in her? Was Franklin encouraging something between her and Jonah because he had already figured out that she was trying to promote something between Esmeralda and Jonah? She had made her life very complicated. But this was no time to abandon her plan.

"Isn't it time to call on Esmeralda, Mr. Finch?" she asked sweetly.

"It's the dinner hour," said Jonah.

"My sister is extremely tired," said Franklin wearily.

"Of course she is," agreed Jonah. "It's been a rough day."

"How do you like Commander Monroe's new buggy, Jonah?" asked Franklin.

"Fine." Jonah looked puzzled.

"Good," Franklin declared. "I'll get it for you. Perhaps you could show Holly—"

"Wait a minute!" she objected. "You just said how tired I was."

"Tomorrow, of course," said Franklin.

"Great idea," agreed Jonah. "I must be going. I'll pick you up one hour after breakfast call. Good evening, Miss Bennington."

Abruptly, he left.

"How could you do that to me?" Holly sputtered at her brother.

"I'm very busy tomorrow. You shouldn't be alone." His eyes darted toward the front door. He was such an inept liar. He hurriedly took Holly inside. He began to explain the layout of the cottage, touting its wooden floors and plastered walls and ceilings as though they were something special.

"You have definitely been in the wilderness a long time," she said.

He didn't wince. He seemed to be building resistance to her comments. He led her down a hallway. The first door on the right was to his bedroom, which he showed her carelessly. It had no more than a brass bed, a wardrobe, and one chest of drawers. Hanging on wall racks were caps, helmets, and sabers.

Franklin smiled as he waved her into a door on the left. She was stunned.

"Franklin! Wherever did you get such a fabulous bed?"

"Do you like it?" he asked.

She walked around the bed, wide-eyed. Its canopy seemed to touch the ceiling. The posts and headboard had roses carved in mahogany. The comforter and canopy were pink and burgundy silk. The feather mattress was so high off the floor she had to step on a small stool and hop up onto it. The bed was as soft as any she had ever felt.

By the bed was a marble-topped stand with a wash basin. Against the wall stood a tall wardrobe of dark purple and black rosewood. A mirror hung the length of its door between carved clusters of grapes. Next to the wardrobe was a dresser of the same rosewood. Above the dresser hung a painting of bright dainty flowers.

It was a warm wonderful bedroom, but Holly got a sick feeling. No man had decorated this room. It had to be the work of Esmeralda. In fact, Franklin had probably borrowed the bedroom suite from the Monroes!

She climbed down from the bed. "The furnishings are nice, for mismatched pieces of Louis XV."

Franklin winced. "You're tired. Come back to the kitchen. We'll eat. The cook is out back, weeding the vegetable garden. In the summer I have him cook early so the kitchen will cool off a little before I eat."

They stepped down into the kitchen. Just inside the door was a table with two chairs. The kitchen smelled of burnt pine. Holly sat down and Franklin brought her a covered plate from a largecast-iron stove. He uncovered the plate with a flourish.

"You remembered!" cried Holly.

"How could I forget how much you loved pot pies, especially beef."

She ran a finger along the scalloped edge of the white plate. "Wherever did you get this ordinary Haviland? From Esmeralda?"

The pie was excellent but not such a distraction that Holly failed to mention Esmeralda in uncomplimentary ways a few more times. After eating, she and Franklin read in the living room until the very mournful notes of a bugle.

Franklin said, "That's taps. Lights out for the troops. And bedtime for me. Enjoy your bath."

"Bath?"

"Yes. Good night."

Holly soon discovered the unseen cook had filled a large tin tub in her bedroom. The warm soapy water was heavenly. Holly wilted as she bathed. She felt as if all her troubles were dissolving in the water.

Squeaky clean and dry, she could barely keep her eyes open long enough to slip on a long cotton gown and crawl between the sheets. She heard nothing until a bugle the next morning. She fought the dawn of a new day. In seconds she was asleep again.

A cannon exploded!

Holly hopped off the bed to peak out her curtains. Forms were hurrying toward the parade ground in the gray light. She heard Franklin thumping around in the next room.

Seconds later, he called, "It's reveille!" The front door slammed.

She dressed in a sage green taffeta.

As she walked into the hallway she heard someone in the kitchen. Every bone in her body wanted to walk to the living room and sit down to wait for Franklin. But she forced herself to walk to the kitchen.

At the wood stove, a Chinese man was frying eggs in bacon grease. He sensed her and turned. He bowed. "Missy hungry?" His eyes were lowered.

"I'll wait for Franklin. Thank you." She was very hungry for eggs, but she scurried back to the living room.

She didn't wait long. A few minutes after Franklin's hall clock struck seven times he was back. During breakfast Franklin perkily detailed how he came to get the services of Hop Fong when he was in Cheyenne. The Chinese man's graceful movement around a stove hid the fact that he had laid rail from San Francisco to Utah. And not so long ago he had still worked in a section gang that repaired railroad track.

Franklin explained, "Hop Fong lives in a room behind the kitchen. He's a very private man."

"So the fewer questions I ask, the better, huh?" chuckled Holly.

Franklin labored over his next words. "A few years ago I would not have bothered to tell you that. But after yesterday I guess I'd better. Surely you will honor my request."

Holly felt a stab of guilt. Her plan leaped into focus. Why did she have to carry it out? But she couldn't back off now. She would never get out of this wilderness. Imagine Franklin touting wooden floors as if they were something special. She would be that backward too if she stayed here very long. She thought of Jonah Finch. He was coming this morning. Her heart skipped! That man was such a nuisance to her. She had forgotten about the buggy ride.

She said, "I don't think I'll go with that Jonah Finch this morning."

"I'm afraid you have to, Holly. It's all set. It would make me look very bad with Colonel Monroe if you failed to take up his hospitality. He's very proud of his buggy."

"Jonah Finch can take Esmeralda."

Franklin set his jaw. "I must get to my post. Jonah will be here in about half an hour. Don't let me down."

That was exactly what she intended to do. What a stir that would cause. But she soon found herself in front of the wardrobe mirror in her bedroom, putting finger puffs in her hair. She would go with Jonah. It would only further her plan. They would probably see Esmeralda. Or perhaps it was best if they didn't see Esmeralda right away. Holly would praise her to the skies for Jonah. Soon he would think Esmeralda the absolute perfection of womanhood. She pulled a strand of hair down past her ear and twirled it until it dangled a perfect ringlet.

Jonah was cheerful when he arrived. He never seemed to have much to do. As the buggy rolled east he named creeks and buttes and other things Holly had no interest in at all. Between these sights of non-interest she spoke casually of the perfect qualities of Esmeralda. The corner of Jonah's mouth finally turned down the tiniest bit as if he were amused.

Suddenly Holly was aware of a sea of tan. "Why we are near some tepees!" she blurted.

"We're going into the Lakota village."

Holly's protest died in her throat. She was too scared to talk. She smelled smoke and things she had never smelled before, not unpleasant but strange. The buggy was soon in the village. Coppery women in buckskin dresses cooked on fires, pounded corn, scraped hides, sewed garments, beaded moccasins, carried children, and did a hundred things Holly couldn't understand at all.

She said in a hopeful voice, "It's strange. They don't seem to take any notice of the buggy."

"They're used to visitors from the camp coming over and gawking around."

"It seems familiar." And then Holly remembered where she had experienced that feeling before. In Philadelphia. At the zoo! The wild animals—no matter how dangerous or hostile they surely must have been in nature—ignored their nosy visitors. These Sioux or Lakotas were also captives!

"I want you to see someone," said Jonah.

"Who?"

"Crazy Horse."

"Crazy Horse!" Wasn't Crazy Horse the Indian who had something to do with the slaughter of General Custer and his men at some place called the Little Big Something? Maybe she was wrong. Maybe she had Crazy Horse mixed up with another chief like Chief Joseph or somebody. It was hard to remember all the chiefs and tribes. Surely she was wrong. Her voice was dry as hot sand. "Were any of these Sioux at the Little Big Something?"

"Just about all of them were at the Little Big Horn."

That outrage took Holly's breath away. She could barely speak. "Do you mean we are riding alone unarmed into the midst of these Sioux who less than one year ago were murdering General Custer and his men?"

"Actually it was General Custer who planned on murdering them."

"I remember now! Isn't this Crazy Horse the Indian no bullet can kill? Isn't he the most hostile of all the hostiles?"

"He's making a nice adjustment."

Holly trembled as they rode ahead. What did Jonah mean when he said she was going to see Crazy Horse? She was afraid to ask. She couldn't remember ever being so afraid. But surely he only meant they would see Crazy Horse from a distance. She was worried over nothing. Of course that was it. His tepee would be far away. Jonah would say, *Look, there he is,* and she would reply, *Where? it's so far away.* And Jonah would say, *The tall one with all the feathers.*

"We're almost there," said Jonah.

"Where?"

"At the lodge of Crazy Horse." He nodded toward a tepee not a stone's throw away. "It's the one with the yellow stripes above the flap door." He leaned over and set the hand brake on the buggy. "The door to a tepee always faces east toward the rising sun—what they see as the source of wisdom."

Now that they were stopped, Holly realized the tepees were three times taller than a man. A man could easily walk around inside without bumping his head. The fierce chief could be inside right this moment pacing around, longing for a walnut-haired scalp of an innocent young lady. He could burst out of the tepee in a flash.

"I don't want to meet Crazy Horse!" she whimpered.

"Oh, he won't talk to you. Or me."

"I don't want to see him either." She could imagine the fierce, vicious face of a relentless savage. She felt thrust into a world before Christ. She would never describe it as Old Testament—that seemed sacrilegious. But deep in her heart, she was afraid that this savage might dazzle her like the angel of light—Lucifer. He might tempt her, deceive her, trick her, accuse her. She must not see him. It would haunt her dreams the rest of her life. She didn't need that. How could Jonah have done such a stupid, insensitive, dangerous thing?

"There he is!" Jonah's voice deepened in awe. "He's coming back to his lodge."

A man approached on foot, wearing a red breechcloth over blue denim pants. High on the sleeves of his white shirt were red garters. His feet wore brown moccasins. There seemed to be nothing on his head. He was wiry and walked very straight, clutching a lance knuckle-tight in one hand. Holly felt herself relax. Could this man be dangerous?

He walked closer. A white choker circled his neck. Suddenly Holly realized the chief's face was young and very light-skinned. His hair was parted in the middle and hung to his waist in long thick braids. And his hair was a soft tan! In his hair were two reddish brown feathers, one straight up and one hanging off to the side.

His eyes were hurt but placid, focused on something a million miles away. He, too, was captive. The chief was a miserably unhappy man.

Holly began to tremble—not from fear but from the thought that she was looking at one of the great warriors of the ages. Seeing Crazy Horse was almost like seeing David. Crazy Horse was a great warrior king who dominated the world of men. And he could do that even though a captive.

Holly stopped trembling, but she felt very sick. It was all too much. No one should take in so much greatness in one day.

"Take me back to the cottage," she whispered shakily.

six

Back at the post Jonah walked Holly to the front door of the cottage. Children were rushing down the road to a small white building Holly knew must be the post school.

"Are you all right?" he asked with unusual sincerity. "You've been white as a sheet since you saw Crazy Horse."

"It's the dry air. I have a headache." Would her lies never end? "I must lie down a while."

"If you'll excuse me, Miss Bennington, I have some things to do. I sure hope you get to feeling—"

"Please go. Call on Esmeralda." Holly shut the door in his face.

She noticed the hall clock said nine o'clock. She was surprised to see a Bible lying open on a table under a kerosene lamp. She hadn't noticed the small table and lamp before. Franklin must have read there last night. The Bible was open to the book of Romans. A bookmark and one of those newfangled pencils lay on the open page. Franklin must have used them to underline the passage.

She read the passage underlined in pencil, "For everything that was written in the past was written to teach us, for that through endurance and the encouragement of the Scriptures we might have hope."

Did Franklin leave that message from Paul for her? It was remarkable. She wanted to read the Scriptures for the first time in many years. In her bedroom she stretched out on the comforter. She hoped Franklin wouldn't come back until after the assembly at sunset. She needed a long time to read—and think. She saw the tin tub was gone. She heard Hop Fong in the kitchen but she knew he would never bother her. And she didn't want to eat lunch.

She read both books of Samuel as voraciously as a lion. Yes, David was a great warrior king. But he had much blood on his hands, too much blood to build the temple! The Old Testament was just as she remembered it. It was very frightening. Fathers tried to kill sons. Sons tried to kill fathers. Wives betrayed their husbands. Husbands betrayed their wives. And death was swift. Who could be as resourceful as Abigail? Who could know if they might not meet death like Uriah, the innocent husband of Bathsheba, or even like Uzzah, who only wanted to keep the Ark from falling? The truths in the Old Testament terrified her.

There was a knock on the front door.

Hop Fong would answer it. But no. He just kept rattling pots around in the kitchen. The knock came again. Should she answer? She knew if she didn't answer the door and the knocker knew Holly was there it would enhance her reputation as a rude nuisance, but somehow she couldn't bring herself to be so unfriendly. The Bible affected her that way. She got up, walked down the hall, and opened the front door.

"Esmeralda!"

"I thought I would call." Esmeralda wore a sweet, dimpled smile. She was dressed in a snug cream poplin. For the first time Holly saw she was robust—small-boned but filled out—the way Holly wished she was filled out herself. Every time Holly thought Esmeralda couldn't possibly be more aggravatingly attractive she was proved wrong.

"Please come in," said Holly without enthusiasm.

Esmeralda stepped in and held Holly's hand. Why was she so personal? Holly wanted to yank her hand away and jump back, but that would be childish. Esmeralda's hand was warm and feathery. Holly was sure her own hand was cold and clammy.

Esmeralda said, "We do a lot of calling here, Holly. We try to be the best of friends. The days and nights are very long here without friends. The worst thing one can do is to do nothing but wait for a new post somewhere else for excitement."

"That's wonderful advice, I suppose. Please sit down." Holly waited for her to sit on one end of the sofa and then sat down on a chair as far from her visitor's warm, grasping hands as possible. "Just what does one do here?"

"We have picnics. We visit the buttes. We watch the gentlemen play a new game called baseball on Sunday afternoons. We ride horses. We visit the Badlands to the north and collect the most mysterious fossils. We work in the Lakota village."

"I was just there." Holly said quickly to stop Esmeralda's list of supposedly wonderful things to do in the wilderness. Immediately, she knew it was a mistake. She didn't want to talk about the village.

"How did you like the Lakota village?" asked Esmeralda.

"It was the most primeval experience of my life." Holly's lip was trembling. "I am still trying to sort it out." She stopped herself. She should have said she was trying to forget it. She was being too honest about it. She would hide behind a lie. "It seems the savage chief Crazy Horse is something of a minor novelty here."

Holly couldn't look Esmeralda in the eye as she said it. She felt very small making Crazy Horse sound trivial. Seeing a great warrior king was one of the most stunning experiences of her life. Now she was belittling it. But she must keep advancing her plan of unrelenting aggravation.

Esmeralda chose her words carefully. "Crazy Horse is special. He's the one Lakota our soldiers admire the most. He's the one chief the Lakota themselves admire the most. He is the most humble. Other chiefs wear war bonnets with long streamers of eagle feathers. He wears two hawk feathers in war or peace. In a sad way, he reminds me of Abraham Lincoln. I feel he is such a great man that he is doomed."

"Doomed?" Holly didn't feel conniving. Would the great chief soon be gone? "I'm sorry."

If only she could speak frankly with Esmeralda. If only she

could tell Esmeralda her real fears and doubts. But how could she now? She had built a very effective fabric of mischief and deceit. What could she do now but continue?

Esmeralda said, "Perhaps you would like to work with some of us in the Lakota village. We work with the Indian agent and the church but we are also very independent."

"I don't believe it is proper to interfere with the superstitions of pagans. I won't preach to them."

Esmeralda moved to the other end of the sofa and took Holly's hand. "Oh, my dear, we don't preach. We are like good wives to them. In First Peter, chapter three, verse one, the apostle said: 'If any of them do not believe the word, they may be won over without words, by the behavior of their wives.'"

"What do you mean? How do you show them your behavior?"

"We behave with 'purity and reverence.' We distribute blankets and clothing. We teach them how to cook with our white flour. We teach them how to make soap. There's so much to do. Crazy Horse's band has only been here one month."

"I don't think I could do that," blurted Holly. Such behavior was dangerously tempting. But if she became active in the Indian village she would never get out of the wilderness. She came so close to liking the idea it made her angry. "By the way, does that Louis XV bedroom suite belong to your father?"

"Yes. Do you like it?"

"I spent a most comfortable night." Why didn't she sneer that it was hopelessly mismatched? Esmeralda just radiated sweetness. But Holly couldn't let herself be foiled by such goodness. She toyed with the frills on her taffeta dress. "Have you seen Jonah Finch today?"

"No, I haven't."

Holly leaned forward in the sly confidential manner she had seen used by the most gossipy young ladies at Gladwyne. "I get the feeling Mr. Finch likes you very much. He shaved off his beard after he saw you."

"How does he look?"

"Marvelous. He has a strong jaw. His upper lip is neither too long nor too short. His lips are not chapped as so many fair-skinned men's are." Holly saw that Esmeralda was hanging on every word. What an opportunity. She would exhaust Mr. Finch. "His skin is ever so lightly freckled, just enough to be charming. His nose is long and straight, very excellent in profile. His eyes, although dark blue, are very lively. His neck for such a tall man is not a turkey neck but very thick and—" Holly stopped. She had said far too much.

"Is there not more you noticed about Mr. Finch?" asked Esmeralda, her eyes wide in wonder.

She must be laughing inside, thought Holly. She would not let Esmeralda enjoy her excessive description of Jonah too much. She would press on. "Jonah Finch is quite a resourceful man I believe. And most interested in you."

A bugle blasted!

"Oh, my word, Holly. It's lunch call. I must be going home. Mother always eats lunch with father. And I must too when I'm in camp."

And suddenly Esmeralda was gone.

Holly had a sick feeling that quick departures always gave her. Did she say something wrong? She laughed aloud. She would have to overcome her shy sensitive ways. After all, she meant to say every thing wrong!

Her strategy depressed her though. Why couldn't she speak of things most profound to her? Why did she have to keep this shallow deception going? Why was such a smarmy deception the only weapon that would get her out of this wilderness?

The front door opened.

"You're back already, Holly?" It was Franklin.

"Yes." She saw Franklin was waiting for her to continue. This was no time to get soft-hearted. She couldn't pass up opportunities. She acted perkily empty-headed. "The buggy ride was short and unpleasant. About the only thing worth remembering was Jonah Finch's desire to spend the rest of the day with Esmeralda."

"Didn't I see Esmeralda leaving our front door?"

"She stopped in for a chat. And then she rushed out in great haste, no doubt to meet Jonah Finch for lunch."

That didn't seem to bother Franklin. Holly had gone too far with that lie. Franklin probably knew Esmeralda always had lunch at home when she was in camp. His eyes swept the room. They seemed to smile as they stopped where the Bible had been lying open. "Your chat was pleasant, I hope," he said cautiously

"More or less."

"Oh." His voice was a groan. "Let's have some lunch."

As they entered the kitchen, Hop Fong was over the stove dishing something from a huge iron skillet onto plates.

Holly was surprised at her plate. "Steak and two eggs for lunch?"

"We eat a lot of beef here. But not the chickens." He laughed.

"Interesting." She schemed as she cut a tiny piece off her steak. "Esmeralda seems taken with Jonah."

"Did she say that?"

"Not exactly. But I can tell there is a mountain of mutual interest between them. And they are a well-matched couple. Don't you agree?"

Franklin sighed. His neck was pink. "Have you been reading the Bible?" He seemed to be praying.

"Some."

"Care to share it's revelation with me?"

"I was reading about David." Why not tell Franklin? Perhaps her terrible distress would win his sympathy. She could tell the truth once in a while. It might even help her. "I was struck with how David and Crazy Horse are great warriors and dreamers."

"Really?" Franklin was pleased.

"It confirms my opinion that this place is right out of the Old Testament." She paused to let the dread sweep over her. It was real enough. "It frightens me. Haven't you always been scared by the Old Testament?"

"I know you have. Don't you remember how you pointed out to me years ago at Mama's funeral that everyone in our family with an Old Testament name was dead but Papa? First Rebecca, then Noah, then Rachel. And of course since Papa died you must feel even stronger about it."

"I don't remember telling you that. I don't even remember thinking that." She really had forgotten it. How sensitive she had been when she was younger. She and Mama had read the Bible every day then. "But what do you think of the Old Testament, Franklin?"

"The facts themselves are scary, I admit. But you must read the Psalms and Isaiah to get the real point."

"And what is the real point?"

"All that turmoil had to happen before Christ came."

"Why?"

"Only God knows why." Franklin seemed edgy. "I must get back to duty. I wish we could talk longer."

Franklin left abruptly, agitated she supposed because he really did want to talk. She took the Bible to the living room and began to read the Psalms. She didn't skip around as she might have when she was younger but started reading aloud right at the beginning.

She finished the first Psalm: "The way of the wicked will perish." It startled her. She reassured herself she herself was not really wicked. Mischievous maybe, but who could blame her for trying to escape such desolation?

She was surprised at how well Psalm two described Christ. But it was written by David, referring to himself. David certainly didn't fulfill it; he was too flawed. It was not fulfilled until Christ. Did David know of Christ? Separated by one thousand years? She remembered something in the book of Matthew. She found it in verse forty-four of chapter twenty-two. Christ himself quoted Scripture:

"The Lord said to my Lord:
    'Sit at my right hand
    until I put your enemies
    under your feet.'
"If David calls him 'Lord' how can he be his son?"

Holly's Bible noted Christ himself was quoting Psalm 110. She read that Psalm. She struggled to understand the promise that David's line would be the line of royal priests forever—the line that would lead to Christ. Christ did not come from the order of Aaron's family in the tribe of Levites, a human lineage of priests, but he came from the mysterious eternal order of Melchizedek.

How well she wrestled the complexities of the Bible. Why had she neglected it so long? She read more Psalms. Her dread left her. She felt the warmth of David's yearning for God, his overwhelming love of God, his unflagging praise of God. She felt the genius of God's thousand-year connection of David with Christ. And what of the thousand-year connection of David with the older, mysterious Melchizedek? God's mastery of human and divine history was overwhelmingly wonderful.

Warnings jumped out at her, too. Psalm 10 said, "The wicked man hunts down the weak, who are caught in the schemes he devises." How was she different? Surely she was not wicked like that!

Psalm eleven said "a scorching wind" would be the lot of the wicked. She squirmed uncomfortably. She had felt that searing wind across the prairie.

She read and reread Psalm eighteen. It seemed the most urgent of David's Psalms. It was fiery and beautiful. She read, "He brought me out into a spacious place; he rescued me because he delighted in me." The "spacious place" struck a chord. That seemed Holly's fate, too. But the spacious place was not punishment. It was rescue. So Holly might be fighting the Lord!

She got on her knees. "Forgive me, Lord." She stopped. She

still wasn't sure what to do. But she knew now where the answers were. She got back up into the chair and read. Passage after passage jolted her. Psalm sixty-eight reminded her that "the rebellious live in a sun-scorched land."

She was immersed in Isaiah when she heard a bugle call at three o'clock. She wasn't sure what the call meant, but she couldn't stop reading about the suffering servant long enough to look out the window.

Whereas before she dreaded the Old Testament, she now delighted in it—the events in it were bringing her straight to Christ and His story in the New Testament. By the time the clock struck five times, she was reading the New Testament. Christ was the answer.

"So this is how you have rescued me, Lord," cried Holly. "Now I must make You delight in me." She thought again of the wonderfully complicated way God controls history. "What if I had not seen Crazy Horse? Surely he was an agent for my change. But I'm certain he could not know that. He is a very great man, but he has to be an unwitting agent in my relationship with God.

"But that is not necessarily true of Jonah!"

Holly jumped up. "Jonah intentionally took me there. But did he do it at the request of Franklin? I must know. If Franklin asked Jonah to do it, then Franklin is inextricably part of God's plan for me. But if Franklin did not ask Jonah to do it, and Jonah did it on his own, how could I doubt that God is using Jonah as part of His plan for me?"

She paced the room. She had to know the answer. She found herself thinking about Jonah a lot. Were those the wandering thoughts of a bored young lady? Or were those God's gentle reminders of Jonah's part in her life?

Through the window she saw a form coming up to the front door. It must be Franklin!

"I must know!" she gasped.

Holly hitched up the hem of her dress and raced to the door.

seven

Holly clutched Franklin by his lapels.

"What's come over you?" he gasped.

"Did you tell Jonah to take me to the Indian village and show me Crazy Horse?"

He laughed nervously. "Did Jonah take you to see Crazy Horse? I wanted to take you there myself." He gently removed her hands from his lapel.

She stumbled back. It was true then. Jonah the roughneck was being used by God in her life. She plopped down on the sofa and threw her head in her hands. What did this mean? And why did she feel at all attracted to such an unfinished person? In seconds she was sobbing.

Franklin sat beside her. "Perhaps seeing Crazy Horse was too much for you too soon."

"It was a mountain peak," she replied, suddenly calm.

Franklin was surprised at her recovery. "Earlier today you told me the ride was short and unpleasant."

"I read the Bible the entire afternoon." She no longer wanted to dwell on the visit to the village.

"Splendid," said Franklin. "Did you read the Psalms and Isaiah?"

"Yes. You gave me excellent advice. I'm getting a much deeper understanding of the New Testament by understanding the Old Testament. Not that I understand everything, of course. But I intend to continue reading the Bible every morning before breakfast and every evening before I retire."

"That's a great idea," Franklin said, his eyes beaming approval and what looked to Holly like relief.

"I'll bet you're relieved that I haven't mentioned Jonah and Esmeralda in the same breath." She felt like abandoning her

65

mischief, but in her heart she knew she couldn't—not quite yet. After all, she was still trapped in the wilderness.

"Relieved but wary." Franklin sounded like a military officer when he said it—tough and brief and concise.

"I'm famished," Holly said, wanting to change the subject.

"Hop Fong has prepared a wonderful beef dish for you. It's my favorite."

"You talk as if you're not eating it with me."

"I'll have only a snack. I have an engagement at the post commander's."

"Oh?"

"I also have to go back to my duties soon. Then after retreat assembly I'll go to the post commander's. I've taken the liberty of asking Jonah to keep you company here after retreat."

"Jonah!" Her heart beat like a trip-hammer. "Why Jonah?"

"Don't you like him?"

"I...I don't know."

"You've been cooped up the entire afternoon. Come on back behind the kitchen. I'd like to show you something."

Holly had avoided the back of the cottage, too afraid she would invade Hop Fong's private domain.

"Why, it's fabulous!" she cried as they stepped outside.

There were more shades of green than she had in her wardrobe. Row upon row of vegetables stretched behind the cottage. Some rows erupted tall and bushy and some rows barely rose above the well-tilled soil. Some rows were hidden under arched papers whose edges were weighted with small rocks or clods.

Franklin pointed. "Peas. Carrots. Lettuce. Beets. Onions. Potatoes. Cabbage. Celery. Spinach. Turnips. Sweet corn. Cucumbers." Then he waved his arm over the huge garden with pride. "And a whole bunch of Chinese vegetables I can't identify unless they are on my plate."

"It's a marvel."

"Hop Fong works very hard in his garden."

"But how does he succeed? It's so hot and dry here."

"The secret is water. Hop Fong spends hours lugging water from the creek." Franklin laughed at a conglomeration of glass bottles and kegs neatly stacked against the back of the cottage. "He must have every spare container in the camp. He straps them on a mule I bought him. He has to keep his mule down at the stables." Franklin pointed at the rows of arched papers. "And another of his secrets is protecting the young sprouts from too much sun until they get sturdier."

"You must have the best garden in the camp."

"Hop Fong has the best garden. Come on back inside. I'll keep you company while you eat. Then I have to go."

Holly glanced around. "Where is Hop Fong?"

"At the post commander's house," answered Franklin with no further explanation.

Holly was silent during supper. Franklin ate a small sandwich and chatted easily about the camp, but she didn't listen. Jonah was coming to keep her company that evening. If only she could figure out why Franklin was constantly pairing her with Jonah. Was it because she had campaigned so blatantly for a match between Jonah and Esmeralda? Was this Franklin's not so subtle way of countering her mischief? Yes, that was undoubtedly the reason.

But how could Franklin put her in the hands of a man who was probably a criminal? Franklin probably forgot Jonah's shady dealings outside the camp. The past was easy to forget inside the camp. Congenial company was rare and Jonah seemed an almost civilized human being in camp.

"I must go now, Holly."

Franklin's words brought her out of her deep thoughts. "The goulash was delicious. But Hop Fong certainly has a light touch with the paprika."

"It was Canton stir-fried beef."

"Oh?" Some dish she had never tasted before? Out here in the wilderness? What irony. She changed the subject. "Now don't worry about me. I'll read the Bible for a while."

After Franklin left, she did read the Bible again. She opened it to Paul's letter to the Romans. She read it for a long time. She wasn't sure if her interpretations of it were true to her own situation or not. But for one moment she was overwhelmed with the desire to spread the good news—just as Paul had done—not to those who already knew of Christ the Messiah but to those with alien gods. Did that mean she must commit herself to saving the Sioux just as Esmeralda did—by example of purity and reverence?

There was a knock on the door. Suddenly Holly realized she had heard a bugle more than once. Was retreat over?

Holly opened the door. There stood Jonah. "It's you," she said flatly.

"Retreat is over," said Jonah. "Won't you join me on the porch?"

"Of course. I have my orders."

"Are you ever not difficult, Holly?"

"Why are you here, Mr. Finch?"

"I see you are in no mood for subtleties. All right, I'll tell you why. The post commander is giving his weekly party. All the officers and their wives and their grown children attend. Franklin did not wish you to jeopardize your future here at the camp when you are in such a…a confused state."

"How awful!"

"Oh, please, don't magnify your plight so much and so often."

"How rude!"

"I thought you wanted the truth."

"I do. But you're brutal."

"Do you know what the physician's wife wrote in her diary at the end of the first day she arrived here at the camp?"

"Of course not."

"She wrote: 'Commenced enjoying the camp. Finished.'"

Holly couldn't keep from laughing. "How could you know what she wrote in her personal diary?"

"Because she tells everyone about it. It's a great joke. Now she loves it here at the camp." He smiled. "I'm only telling you this so you'll know your reaction is not unusual at all. But when you're in such an unhappy mood, you should not mix with folks who might have forgotten how unhappy they were when they first came here."

"I believe this is all to protect Franklin's career."

"That's not true, but I wouldn't mind if it were. Franklin's career should be protected. The peacetime army doesn't give many promotions, Holly. I'll tell you what a great change has happened. In 1865 a million soldiers were in uniform. Now there are only twenty thousand."

"How do you know so much about the army?"

He ignored her question. "We have a couple hours before Franklin returns. Let me tell you about the camp. Then when you go to your first party you'll be known as a wise woman."

Holly resisted a sharp reply. She realized she really did need to know about the camp. She had been so selfish she had hardly asked a single question that didn't spring from her plans to escape the wilderness.

"All right," she said, folding her hands. "Tell me about the camp."

"First commandment for a tranquil life at this post: don't discuss politics or Custer. You may think the room will be equally divided on these subjects, but every one in the room will finds fault with anything you say because they feel so strongly about the subject."

"And religion?"

"Be your own counsel. I don't feel right about waving anyone off religion."

"What have you become, Mr. Finch, some kind of prairie philosopher?"

"You will find much discussion here of many subjects. We may not have libraries and colleges, but human thought is very portable."

"My." For once Holly spoke with true admiration.

"I've became a regular windbag—like Blabby."

"Is that unusual for you?"

"Very."

"I'm flattered." She would ask Franklin later if Jonah's reticence to talk was true.

He cleared his throat. She could tell the conversation had been much more personal than he intended. He said, "Colonel Monroe is the post commander. He has about a thousand officers and soldiers under him. There are parts of three regiments: the Fourteenth Infantry and the Ninth Infantry and the Third Cavalry. The infantrymen are foot soldiers, what the Indians call 'walk-a-heaps.' Cavalrymen ride horse. Your brother is in the 3rd Cavalry."

"He is?" She felt shame at being so ignorant.

"The 3rd Cavalry has a long tradition. It was organized as the 1st Mounted Rifles in 1846 for the Mexican War. At full strength it has twelve companies, sometimes called troops. Each troop is supposed to have one captain, one first lieutenant, one second lieutenant, one first sergeant, one quartermaster sergeant, four sergeants, eight corporals, two musicians, two blacksmiths, one saddler, and eighty-four privates."

"I believe you are betraying yourself, Mr. Finch. You must have been kicked out of the cavalry."

"Pshaw. Everybody on every post in the frontier knows what I just told you."

"Tell me again," she asked.

She listened to him repeat the roster. Then he added, "There are about a hundred men in a company or troop. But usually in these days troops are only half filled. In fact Franklin is really the acting captain of Troop A. To make a long windy story short, the 3rd Cavalry has about six hundred men, twelve troops of about fifty men."

"How do you tell these men apart?"

"Yellow stripes on the pants are cavalry. White, infantry." Jonah continued a long monologue on how to distinguish different regiments and different ranks by their uniforms. Holly didn't interrupt. She soaked up as much as she could. And she noticed Jonah felt comfortable relating the information in a detached way. She didn't miss the opportunity to study his face. He was such an enigma. He had such a good face. But, she supposed, so did Jesse James.

"When are you going to level with me, Jonah Finch?" Her frankness shocked her.

"What do you mean, ma'am?"

"You are telling me all this, just so you won't have to talk about yourself."

"Not true, ma'am. I'm telling you all this, so you won't embarrass yourself. You're much too young with far too many years ahead of you to do that. And besides, you're much too nice."

"Don't try to distract me with flattery." Inside she felt the joy of a million butterflies. "Tell me about yourself."

"Oh, that's no great secret."

"Then tell me. I want to know everything!" She felt herself blush at her own eagerness. And she sounded so coquettish.

"I was born over Illinois way."

"A Westerner!"

"Western Illinois," answered Jonah and he laughed. "Why I could see the Mississippi River from our front porch. My pa farmed the bluffs southeast of a village called New Boston."

"It must have been terribly wild."

"Illinois may seem that way to you, ma'am, but Illinois was tame by the time I was a boy. Abe Lincoln himself surveyed and laid out our town years before I was born. Oh, we had a family of Blackhawk Indians living near our farm. In fact, I played with a boy named Blue Wolf. I almost got to thinking like an Indian, but they moved. I can't remember why anymore. We may have cut down a tree. Or we may have raised too much dust harvesting wheat."

"So are you a farmer?"

"I would have been happy to be just that, ma'am. It's a very honorable thing to do."

"But?"

"Pa had a cousin, Judge Hiram Thornton, who talked me into going to school back east."

"You've been back east?"

"Yes, ma'am.

"College?"

"Yes, ma'am."

"What did you study?"

"Mathematics, French, engineering, some other subjects."

"Do you mean you are an engineer?"

"No, ma'am."

Suddenly the truth struck her. She felt foolish. "You were a cadet at West Point, weren't you?"

"Yes, ma'am."

"Franklin was there, too. Were you classmates, Mr. Finch?"

"No, ma'am. Your brother was just coming in to West Point as I was going out."

"Why did you leave the army?"

"It's hard to explain, ma'am. But even Ulysses Grant left the service, you know."

"Yes, but he returned to become a great general and president."

"The War of the Rebellion forced that. This is peacetime."

"Peacetime seems a poor excuse to become a shady drifter."

"Are you trying to provoke me, ma'am?"

"Not at all." But she had. Suddenly she felt very sneaky and conniving again. Surely Jonah was not telling her the whole truth. Why should she abandon her wonderful plan? She added nonchalantly, "I saw Esmeralda today."

"I'm glad. She's very nice."

"She said you had picnics together."

"She did, huh?" He grinned.

"She said you visit the buttes together."

"Beautiful, aren't they?" He chuckled.

"Apparently you play a new game called baseball on Sunday afternoons as Esmeralda watches."

"Baseball is catching on as a summer pastime."

"Do you ride horses together?" There was some anger in her voice.

"Not often—if at all." He laughed.

"I suppose you visit the Badlands to the north with her and collect mysterious fossils."

"If we do, I've forgotten."

"I know better than ask if you work in the Lakota village with her."

"How did you know about that?"

"You do?" Holly felt anger warm her. It had started out as

mischief. She was supposed to encourage Jonah and Esmeralda. Where had it gone wrong? The thought of Jonah and Esmeralda together made her very angry.

"You two are certainly deep in conversation." The voice came out of the darkness. It was Franklin speaking as he came up the walk. Holly hadn't noticed him coming.

"Did you have a pleasant evening?" asked Jonah in a relieved voice.

"It was a pleasure." Franklin said it with conviction.

"Goodnight." And Jonah nodded politely to Holly and abruptly walked away.

"Thank you for visiting me!" Holly was stunned by his quick departure. She turned to Franklin. "Was I only a chore for Jonah?"

"Shall we go inside?" he answered.

"Of course." She stared numbly as Jonah walked away into the night.

Inside, Franklin yawned. "It's a been a long day. And reveille is very early. I'm turning in."

She blurted, "Is Jonah a big talker?"

He laughed. "Why no. Getting words out of Jonah is about as likely as getting a warm breeze in January."

Her heart soared. "Do you suppose I could go with Esmeralda tomorrow to the village?" She was surprised. The question came from deep inside her soul so suddenly. Why did she want to go?

"Of course!" answered Franklin. His energy was instantaneous. "I'll go tell her at once. I may not have a chance to tell her before she leaves for the village in the morning." He suddenly stopped by the door. "Say, this isn't just an opportunity for you to—"

"Create some mischief?" Holly laughed. She felt so wonderful. "Yes."

"Why would you think so?" Her heart was beating fast. She added, "Won't we need a driver? Perhaps Jonah could drive us."

"You'll certainly need a driver." Franklin took a deep breath and left.

eight

So she had done it!

The plea to go to the village with Esmeralda had come straight from her heart. But what did it mean? She was so confused. Why had she asked for Jonah? Was she going to continue to play Cupid between Esmeralda and Jonah? Or had she really done it so she could be near Jonah? Suddenly she felt fluttery. What was this sensation? Desire? Surely not. How could she think such a thing? She had never felt like this before. She was tingling with anticipation. She had seen that heightened excitement in some of the young ladies at Gladwyne, but she had never understood it—until now.

Holly tried to push her feelings for Jonah aside. They were too strong. They frightened her. She busied herself looking in her luggage. The first light-colored poplin or calico dress she could find would be the dress she would wear the next morning. She didn't want to disturb her luggage too much. It was nicely packed to go right back east at the first available opportunity. Would she ever wear her fancy silks and satins again? Yes, if she could get her wardrobe and herself out of the wilderness.

She found a creamy poplin dress and a straw hat to match. She was hanging the poplin in the wardrobe in her bedroom when someone rapped on her door.

"Still up?" It was Franklin.

"Yes, what is it?"

"You are all set to go with Esmeralda to the village right after breakfast. Good night."

But what about Jonah? She wanted to ask but stopped herself. She would sound too anxious. Why was her heart beating so fast? Surely Jonah would drive them. And asking Franklin about Jonah would upset him. Holly read her Bible again.

Sleep that night was sweet for Holly. She could hardly remember a time it had been such a comfort. Maybe when Mama was still alive—when Holly felt very good about herself most of the time.

The next morning after breakfast she went to the porch with Franklin and watched him stride across the parade grounds. The entire morning she had bit her tongue. She so wanted to ask Franklin if Jonah were driving her and Esmeralda. The thought of being near Jonah was delicious—too delicious for Holly to analyze. She found herself relishing the thought of Jonah, but also skirting any reflection on what it meant. The answer might shock her.

She sat in a wicker chair and watched Franklin walk across the parade ground and finally disappear inside one of the long buildings Holly knew were the stables. Seconds later Esmeralda was coming up the walk toward the cottage.

Esmeralda waved. "Praise the Lord for a good morning. I'm so glad you decided to go with me."

"Thank you. I'm ready," answered Holly nervously.

"Here comes the buggy."

Holly gawked at the approaching buggy. Her heart was soaring. What was happening to her? "Who's driving?" she asked breathlessly.

"Oh, good. Our driver is Billy Boudreau."

"The trader's son?" asked Holly, her voice hiding her disappointment.

Esmeralda laughed. "Yes. He's sixteen—a boy back east in a city like Philadelphia, but a man here." She waved toward the buggy. "Hello, Billy!"

Billy jumped down from the buggy. "Morning."

Holly smiled at him. There was no point in taking her disappointment out on a boy. "Good morning, Billy."

"Morning," he grunted.

Holly relaxed as Billy flicked the reins and the buggy rolled toward the village. Her anticipation at seeing Jonah now seemed silly. What had come over her? She must be suffering from some mild form of hysteria caused by too much prairie dust and sun. She had to concentrate on other things. She studied Esmeralda, who wore a straw bonnet and a pale yellow dress of some kind of coarse tufted fabric Holly couldn't recognize.

Finally Holly said, "Would it be rude of me to ask what fabric your dress is made of?"

"I made it," answered Esmeralda calmly.

"You're a good seamstress. It's a very snug fit." Holly tried to keep the envy out of her voice. Esmeralda filled her dress the way Holly wished she could fill a dress. What man would notice Holly next to Esmeralda? And in her deepest thoughts she realized she was wishing Jonah would not see Esmeralda next to herself. She should be very thankful Jonah was not there.

"Yes, I cut it and sewed it together," answered Esmeralda, lightly interrupting Holly's hot swirling thoughts. "But I also meant that I made the fabric."

"You wove the cloth!"

"Yes," answered Esmeralda proudly. "It's wool. Not the best thing for summer but I never wear any dress to the village that I didn't make myself from scratch. I sheared the sheep myself. I cleaned the wool myself and carded it. And I colored the yarn with a dye the Lakota showed me how to make from tree bark."

Holly felt Esmeralda's sleeve. "It's wool?"

"A very loose twill weave. It isn't that hot really. No fabric feels cool here in the summer when it gets up to a hundred degrees."

"How many dresses have you made like this?"

"Including dresses the Lakota showed me how to make from cow hide, I have about ten dresses. But I mainly wanted to make dresses from wool so I could show the Lakota how to do it. The growing season is too short here for cotton, but the Lakota can easily raise sheep in this country, if only I can convince them it's worthwhile."

"Aren't you interfering with their customs?"

"We've already done that. They built their life around the buffalo. But those days are almost gone. I can only offer them alternatives. They don't have to take them. In fact, a Lakota can be just as stubborn about changes as we whites are."

"Oh?" Did Esmeralda mean Holly? It seemed like she looked at Holly in a pointed way. Holly would change the subject. "And did you make your bonnet?"

"Yes. The Lakota showed me how to weave grass."

"All my things are ready made," said Holly.

"Oh, my dear. Don't concern yourself so soon." Esmeralda put her hand on Holly's arm. "You take your time deciding what you want to do here."

Billy stopped the buggy in front of a large log building at the edge of the Lakota village. "We're here," he grunted.

Esmeralda explained, "That small building yonder is the office of the Indian Agent. This large building belongs to the agency trader. There are our ladies."

At least thirty Indian women were standing and sitting along the side of the trader's building.

"Why, they are wrapped in blankets up to their eyes," Holly exclaimed.

"It's a form of modesty. Or privacy. Even a Lakota brave might do that if he wants to be left alone. A stranger could walk through the village wrapped up that way and not one Lakota would bother him."

"What a nice custom."

They climbed down and Holly stood by dumbly as Esmeralda spoke for several minutes in a language completely unknown to her. Some Lakota children were held by the women, but many were dashing all about. The boys were very rough.

Finally Esmeralda turned to Holly. "I introduced you, and I told them today we would make things with the white flour the government issues them."

Holly watched Esmeralda explode into piling firewood, mixing flour and water, whipping the mixture, all the while speaking what had to be Lakota. It sounded Scandinavian to Holly. Some of the lighter-skinned Lakota women even looked Scandinavian, and Holly was stunned by how peculiar that was. One woman looked like Hop Fong's sister.

A small girl sauntered around Holly. She was about four or five years old. Her dark eyes were very bright and she couldn't stop smiling.

Holly said, "Why, I know you! I met you when you were with Jonah."

"She's my squirt cousin," grunted Billy, who sat on the ground, leaning against the buggy wheel.

The small girl held her hands in front of her face. And then she held her right hand against her heart and threw her hand level and out to the right.

"Why, the little darling is playing a game with me," said Holly.

"She's talking to you," explained Billy.

"Sign language! How wonderful! What did she say to me in Lakota?"

Billy scowled. "Sign language is good with all tribes who follow the buffalo—not just Lakota."

"Oh. A universal language?" She waited in vain for Billy to answer, then asked, "What did she say to me?"

Billy sighed. "Nothing much. She says you are very pretty."

How wonderful! And how forgiving. Holly still wanted to makeup to the little girl for spoiling her visit with Jonah. Holly pointed at the small girl, put her hands in front of her face, then put her right hand over her heart and flung it out. The small girl's eyes laughed and she shuffled her feet shyly.

"The precious little dear." Holly burned to know everything the small girl was thinking. "What is her name in signs?" She didn't want to admit she forgot the girl's name.

Billy grumbled, "Hey, squirt." He held his right hand out, palm forward. His thumb and fingers were spread and pointed up at the sky. He wiggled his right hand left and right, then pointed at the little girl with his left hand. When he saw the little girl was paying attention, he crooked his index finger and thumb together on his right hand and placed them by his mouth. Then he straightened his index finger and flung his hand out.

The little girl quickly rubbed her face and signed something else with both arms so fast Holly couldn't tell exactly what she did.

"Her name is Red Wing," Billy explained.

"Which woman is her mother?"

"She will be with her grandmother."

Holly gasped. "Is her mother dead?"

"No. A little girl like that stays with one of her grandmothers most of the day."

"Why?"

"Because her mother is very hard with her." Billy shook his head. Did this white woman know nothing?

Holly wanted to know all these things now. What did it all mean? How she longed to speak to little Red Wing. She must learn sign language. Holly could talk to any Indian in the plains that way. Then she must learn Lakota. Why, she might even teach a little girl like Red Wing to speak English. Of course, she must do that. Had she forgotten so soon how she wished her father had sent her to school years earlier than he did?

She couldn't keep silent. "I'm going to come here every day from now on."

"Sure," said Billy skeptically.

But after that day, Holly went to the village with Esmeralda every day except Sunday. She burned with fiery righteousness inside as she mixed batter and baked bread. She stole some of Hop Fong's secrets and helped Esmeralda and the Lakota women in the huge garden they were trying to cultivate behind the trader's building. Soon the Lakotas were hoarding containers too and using them daily to feed precious water to their tender plants.

Holly's own secret plan to teach Red Wing English grew to include all the Lakota children. She remained silent about her ideas, though. Every day she learned more signs, more of the Lakota spoken language, and more about the Lakotas themselves.

Red Wing sauntered over to Holly every day. When she held Holly's hand and leaned against her leg, Holly's heart melted.

One day as Esmeralda was pouring a carefully measured amount of water into a trough full of ashes, she said to Holly, "It's so nice of you to be a friend to Red Wing. She doesn't have a sister and she has only one brother. She's going through a very difficult time."

"How do you mean that?"

"Her brother just reached the age where he can longer speak directly to his sister. And of course Billy doesn't want to either. Red Wing feels so lonely."

"I didn't know they had that custom. Why didn't Billy tell me that?"

"Billy doesn't complain and he doesn't explain." Esmeralda paused. "Anyway, at about seven, a boy can no longer speak directly to any woman, even his mother. Lakota are very strict about relationships between men and women, boys and girls. A man is not allowed to look at his mother-in-law. Every effort is made to avoid temptation."

"Do they have such rigid laws?" asked Holly, not expecting an answer. Why had she thought Esmeralda was oblivious to the customs of the Lakotas? It was Holly who was ignorant. But she would not stay that way.

Changing the subject, Esmeralda laughed and commented, "You don't know how difficult it is to get the soldiers to go up and cut bur oak in the Black Hills."

"Why must we use the ashes of bur oak to make the lye that makes the soap?"

"It's the only white oak that grows around here. Hickory would do as well, but it grows even farther away. Eventually I guess the Lakotas must use local wood, but the soap will not be as good."

"Red Wing says her grandmother washes her hair with the

roots of something called *hupa stola*."

"That's the yucca plant. It grows all over the prairie." Esmeralda knelt down to survey a second trough under the trough of ashes. "We have a lot of lye now." She placed an uncooked egg in the liquid. It bobbed on the surface. "Perfectly good and thick too. We'll make soap this week. But let's wait until after the party tomorrow night. Making soap could keep us here late."

The weekly party at the post commander's house! Holly had forgotten. Would Esmeralda ask her if she was going? Holly quickly gushed, "At last we will get to boil the lye and dump in all the beef fat the women have saved! I feel like I am rediscovering all the great secrets of women through the ages. I was so sheltered. I can hardly believe such a concoction makes soap."

Esmeralda lowered her eyes. "I do hope you will like our party."

How could Holly answer her? Franklin probably wasn't going to take her. Suddenly she realized Red Wing was tugging on her arm. "What is it?" asked Holly, grateful for the distraction.

"You me go home."

"Home?" Holly knew exactly what Red Wing meant and she was scared. But if she went with Red Wing, maybe Esmeralda would forget to ask her again about the party. She turned to Esmeralda. "Don't you think I should go with Red Wing?"

"Yes. It will be all right," said Esmeralda. "Her tepee is only about a quarter of mile from here. She wants you to see where she lives."

Holly was frightened walking through the village. She smiled at every Lakota she saw. The men threw blankets up in front of their faces. The women watched without expression. Finally Red Wing stopped on the east side of a tepee. The flap was open. She bent down and peeked in.

Red Wing signed to Holly.

"Empty?" asked Holly. She felt sick, but she crawled inside

after Red Wing and then stood up.

Light streamed down from the gaping smoke hole at the top of the poles. Holly saw the summer-dead fire in the middle of the tepee. Red Wing stood on the left side of the fire. Holly took one step toward the right.

"No!" Red Wing hurried to take her arm.

In her simplest Lakota, Red Wing explained the blanket on the far west side, farthest from the door, was where her father slept. The blankets on the south side were where she and her mother slept and a blanket on the north side was where her brother slept. Red Wing stomped her feet to make it clear no woman or girl walked on the north side of the tepee.

"And I'm sure no man or boy walks on the south side of the tepee. So many rules," said Holly aloud. "Where does your grandmother sleep?" Holly made the sign for 'mother' by tapping her breast twice and added the sign for 'old' by motioning with her right hand like she walking with a stick. Then Holly shrugged questioningly.

Red Wing laughed with glee and pointed to a rolled blanket just south of the flap. Yes, grandmother slept in front of the flap at night.

Holly laughed with glee, too. "Any intruder has to try to slip past your light-sleeping, thunder-tongued grandmother, Red Wing!"

How Holly began to love Red Wing and the ways of the Lakotas. How could anyone regard them as savages?

That evening as they rode back to the camp in the buggy, Holly remembered the post commander's party. She was sure Franklin wouldn't take her. And to prevent Esmeralda from remembering the party, Holly kept up a constant chatter about Lakota words and customs.

As Holly walked up to the cottage she sang out to Esmeralda in a voice light and cheery with relief, "Good night."

Esmeralda called out, "Franklin told me he was looking forward to taking you to the party tomorrow!"

nine

Holly rushed into the office where her luggage was kept.

"Oh, my word. What must Franklin think?"

Canvas bags and cardboard boxes were opened and gaping all over Franklin's study. She had enjoyed the spectacle at first. The chaos surely reminded Franklin every day how rash he was to auction off Mama's Saratoga trunks and nearly all the rest of their belongings. And the concentrated disarray was practical. She could make a quicker escape when her time came to leave the wilderness.

There was one disadvantage. Holly had to rummage through the chaos of luggage every day for things to wear. Perhaps she really ought to hang a tiny fraction of her clothing in her wardrobe. It certainly wouldn't mean she had decided to stay. Granville's letter offering her a job would come any day now.

"Bye-bye, wilderness," she sang aloud.

But she would go ahead this once and hang up some of her dresses. It was no more than a practical way of sorting through her clothes to select the right dress for the party. She looked forward to running her hands over nice satins and silks. For days she had worn nothing but calicos and poplins, except for one gingham dress Franklin brought her from the post trader's store.

"How do you like this garment, Miss Bennington?" she asked herself as she whisked a sea green watered silk from a box. "It's ever so nice. But no. It's too safe. I feel more daring. I feel so daring I might even wear the velvet and satin plum!"

Oh, did she dare? She had only worn the velvety satin plum dress once. And she had never ventured in it beyond her dressing room mirror. The skirt was so splendid with shiny tiers of

83

satin festooned with intricate ruffles. And the top! Simple, snug velvet with no sleeves. The most wonderful ruffly satin collar made it perfect. There was only one problem: Holly. The plum dress was a dress for a woman, not a girl.

"I am a woman!" she snapped.

She ran into her bedroom. Within minutes she had changed into billowy party undergarments and nervously pulled on the plum dress. The top still felt loose. Who was she fooling? In two years she hadn't changed a bit. She zipped the dress up the side.

She took a deep breath and in tiny steps approached the purple and black rosewood wardrobe. The long mirror hung the length of its door between carved clusters of grapes. And what would Holly look like in the dress? A prune?

Holly peeked timidly at the mirror. Her mouth hung open in amazement. Was it possible? She filled the dress. An artist could not have painted a better fit.

"Holly?"

It was Franklin out in the hallway. Would he confirm her invitation to the party? Maybe Esmeralda was wrong. Oh, how could she be so pessimistic? She called confidently, "I'm picking a dress for the party tomorrow."

"Oh," he said. "That's nice."

Somehow she found his male indifference endearing, even encouraging. He didn't sound at all worried. Holly herself felt increasingly nervous about the upcoming party, and sleep did not come easily.

It was a good thing Holly went to the village the next day and worked with the Lakotas. Otherwise she might have been fretting the entire day. Mama had always told her it was not good to stew over things no matter how important they were. It showed a lack of trust in God. So it was nice to have something to do.

That evening Franklin was already at the cottage when Holly returned. "Come back to the kitchen and eat with me, Holly." The fare was tea and sandwiches of thin-sliced cold beef on buttered bread. It was completely unlike Hop Fong to prepare such a light meal. Franklin explained. "This is a snack. We'll be eating at the party, but not for several hours. Hop Fong is over at the post-commander's kitchen right now. All the cooks pitch in to get the food ready for the weekly party." He acted nervous.

"Oh?" replied Holly casually. All day she had denied how important the party was for her future—and Franklin's. Now reality erupted a thousand butterflies inside her. She closed her eyes. *Trust God,* she reminded herself.

After the snack she was too busy getting ready to fret. She bathed in her bedroom and washed her hair and brushed it until her arms were aching. She parted her hair in the middle and pulled it back over her ears. Then she pulled a few strands forward and crimped them, so they would dangle by her cheeks. She arranged her long hair in back in a "beaver tail" held together by fine transparent net. The red tones in her hair never looked sunnier.

In her ears were small, deep purple amethysts encircled with pearls. A tiny lavender headband matched lavender suede gloves that came up past her elbow. The dress was just as she thought the day before. Perfect. She had worried some during the day. She had fleeting dark moments when she thought she had judged herself in the mirror the previous evening too hastily and much too generously. But no, the upper part of the dress fit her curves perfectly. When did she get curves?

Franklin's reaction to Holly's appearance reassured her. "I'm stunned. How can I ever say 'little sister' again? That's just a memory."

They were among the first at the post commander's house. This was a great relief to Holly. It seemed so much easier to meet people a few at a time. Arriving last in the midst of forty people would have been overwhelming to her. She really was very relaxed being introduced to everyone a few at a time. She was even relaxed meeting Colonel Monroe and his wife. The sweet disposition and poise of Esmeralda helped, too. She was a rock for Holly.

Holly really began to feel like she belonged. Jonah's coaching had helped her confidence, too. Her few moments with Colonel Monroe visibly impressed him. He admitted he was taken aback by her knowledge of the camp and the Lakota village.

"Esmeralda said you were a diligent worker," he remarked, "but apparently I was too dense to realize she was also telling me you are a very acute observer. Your sharp eyes are a welcome addition to the camp to be sure." He seemed to want to add something more but bit his tongue. He set his face in stone and forced himself to look away.

Holly soon learned that socializing between men and women was very complimentary but also very brief. The party seemed to have a ritual politeness between men and women that was not allowed to go much further than an exchange of a few compliments. Even Esmeralda and Franklin parted company after only a few minutes of conversation. Holly soon found herself alone, but she was quickly rescued by the colonel's wife.

"Well, my dear," said Mrs. Monroe, "have you conquered your blues?"

"Blues?" Holly was startled, then embarrassed. Were her antics common knowledge?

"Oh," said Mrs. Monroe as she put her hand on Holly's arm, just as Esmeralda always did, "you would be an odd duck indeed if you immediately liked it here. I've been in Army camps off and on for twenty-five years, and at each new camp I feel positively lower than a snake for a few days."

"You do?"

"Of course, my dear. That's why these weekly get-togethers are so terribly important. It's human nature to want to be reassured that everything is all right, that everything is as it should be. Even the Lakotas do it. Every year during the full moon of June they hold their great sundance festival."

"It sounds very gala."

"It's not, my dear." Mrs. Monroe leaned forward very confidentially and lowered her voice. "The dance around the sundance pole is a ghastly sight you will never want to see. Brave men torture themselves in a way that I could not find words to describe. The colonel will have to hog-tie me to get me back there. I was just making a point. The only thing worth remembering about the sundance festival I squirmed through was the strange chief Crazy Horse."

"Yes. He is so strange, isn't he?"

"I imagine you saw him in his usual trance-like stupor. But I saw something quite amazing."

"Oh? Please tell me about it."

"At the sundance festival, the Lakotas were to engage in a mock battle re-enacting the Little Big Horn Battle between the Lakotas and General Custer. It was certainly in terribly bad taste, but I think maybe some of our officers put them up to it, hoping they could learn more truth about what happened during the battle. At any rate Crazy Horse's men, who had just arrived at the camp a few weeks before and were still wilder than buffalo, were given the role of the Lakotas in the battle. And the Lakotas we call the friendlies, the ones who hang around forts, were given the role of Custer and his men. Well, it turned out to be an astonishingly stupid idea because apparently there is murderous hostility between these two groups of Lakota anyway. The mock battle became a real battle. It was terrifying. The colonel says the Lakotas are the most fierce light cavalry in the world. And there I was, sitting in a chair, sipping lemonade like a silly bumpkin and watching several thousand Lakota on horseback turning the game into a real battle. I noticed several Lakota brandishing war clubs and knives. Suddenly shots were fired. I thought we ladies were sure to die."

"That's unbelievable," gasped Holly.

"That's what I thought. But it was real enough."

"What happened?"

"Crazy Horse left the circle of chiefs and walked right out into the middle of the raging dusty battle with horses skimming past him on every side."

"Ahhhh." Crazy Horse again, thought Holly. Doing something that defied reality. Such men did exist. She had to blink her eyes to keep from crying.

Mrs. Monroe didn't notice the young woman's excitement. She shook her head and held out her hands. "He laced the fingers of both hands together like this and held his hands high in the air. It was some kind of signal. And suddenly every horse was dead still. Dust hung in the air. The battle was over. I've never seen a display of primitive power like that. And I never want to see it again."

Holly said diplomatically, "I can understand your concern." But how she wanted to see such power. Crazy Horse had made the sign every Indian on the plains knew meant "peace." But when Crazy Horse made the sign, it became a command. And his command shot through thousands of rampaging angry Lakota like lightning through a hail storm.

"Oh, I'm depressing you," said Mrs. Monroe. "Just take my advice: Don't go to a sundance. Perhaps you could tell me about your work in the village."

Holly began to suspect she was Mrs. Monroe's ward for the evening. Or was it a normal feeling-out process? Would Mrs. Monroe dutifully report her findings to the colonel later? No doubt. Well, two could play that game.

Holly asked, "Do you know Jonah Finch well?"

"Jonah who?"

"Jonah Finch. Esmeralda seems to know him well."

"Is he one of the new officers?"

"No, ma'am. I don't believe so." Holly was taking a risk now. That answer was a deliberate deception. She should have smiled and said, *No, ma'am. He's a civilian,* but she was too curious about Jonah.

"Is he an older man?"

"Late twenties. Red hair. Tall. Broad-shouldered. Eyes as azure as the morning sky."

"Why, that adorable man sounds like...oh, he couldn't be.

Of course not. That young officer was with us way back in '71—in Arizona. I haven't seen him since." The smile faded from her lips. "But it doesn't matter. He couldn't be who you are talking about."

"What is his name?"

"Why, my dear, I've quite forgotten." But Mrs. Monroe looked just as sober as if she had remembered everything she wanted to remember.

"Do you get around the camp much, Mrs. Monroe?"

"I must confess I'm a stay-at-home. No, I don't go out much. I go out only on semi-official functions with the colonel. I certainly don't go into the countryside with the gunrunners about and the whiskey-runners about and the miners sneaking gold back from the Black Hills and the horse thieves—"

"Horse thieves too?" Holly's question sounded silly because it was as if gunrunners and whiskey-runners and miners were too common to question.

"Terrible men are stealing the Lakota horses and selling them in Sidney."

"I didn't know it was so dangerous in the countryside."

"Oh, it isn't for an athletic young lady like yourself with the proper escort but," and once again she placed her hand on Holly's arm, "does this body look like it's made for fleeing?"

Mrs. Monroe was nearly as wide as she was tall. Holly groped for words. "I'm sure you're quite speedy."

Mrs. Monroe laughed. "Oh, you are very speedy, too, my dear. Especially up here." And she tapped her head.

Suddenly the party swarmed around a piano and they sang songs. A captain with family roots in Switzerland played the zither. They ate smoked oysters and tiny ham sandwiches before vanilla ice cream. All marveled over how ice cream could be made even in the frying heat of the summertime. One officer took a deep bow. Mrs. Monroe explained to Holly that the officer was the mastermind who sawed great blocks of ice from the river in January and stored them between layers of straw in a deep excavation just north of the post-commander's house.

In the middle of summer they pulled blocks of ice from the deep hole and made ice cream.

Holly enjoyed the party. Once or twice she felt a twinge of regret that Jonah couldn't be there. Surely he would like the way Holly looked tonight. But Mrs. Monroe was easy to talk to, even if Holly might be her chore for the colonel. And she met several other officer's wives. She learned that only she and Esmeralda were working in the village. The other wives did token work. And Holly learned there was a great resistance to understanding the Lakotas. It was not a Christian aversion to pagan rites. It was very un-Christian. It was a deep distrust of aliens. Holly would remember that. Some of these wives would not understand her enormous affection for Red Wing.

Were the officers that way, too?

In the cottage after the party, Holly asked Franklin, "Are you officers learning the customs of the Lakota?"

"We employ scouts for that. It is not good policy to openly appreciate their culture—although most of the men really do admire the Lakotas. We want them to adopt our culture."

"But Esmeralda isn't that way."

"Isn't she? What does she do at the village?"

"She is teaching them how to take advantage of our ways."

"Exactly."

"That's cynical, Franklin."

Holly prayed Esmeralda was not calculating like that. Esmeralda was showing the Lakota how wonderfully a woman in Christ behaved. And Holly prayed she wouldn't allow the calculating attitude of a few in the camp poison her feelings for the Lakotas. If they were really converting Lakotas into apples—red on the outside and white on the inside, like Billy Boudreau once said—Holly didn't want to stay in the wilderness. The Lakotas were wonderful people who could be more wonderful in Christ, while remaining Lakotas. After all, Germans were Germans and Swedes were Swedes, weren't they?

In the days after the party, Holly continued to go to the village with Esmeralda every day except Sundays. She also stayed at camp on the first Wednesday in July when the entire camp celebrated Independence Day with a gigantic picnic and wondrously loud fireworks.

The Lakota women were friendlier to her. Billy Boudreau said the sullen Lakota women had seen many white women come for a few days and then never return. Holly was even more determined to be one of the rare ones like Esmeralda—a real hard-working friend who would show them how to make soap or make cloth or grind corn into cornmeal with a mechanical grinder.

Holly soon felt like a veteran at the post-commander's weekly party. She knew what to talk about and what not to talk about. And they touched her heart one week by honoring her one-month anniversary at the camp! Franklin also took her to her first regimental party in July. Noncommissioned officers and soldiers of the Third Cavalry cleared their barracks of bunks and footlockers and decorated the ceiling and walls with brightly colored crepe. It was all Holly could do not to be consumed by pride. The eyes of every bachelor in the 3rd Cavalry told her she was a great prize!

Once in a while she remembered her scheme to extract a letter from Granville Wiggins III so she would have an excuse to leave the wilderness. But the letter never came. And she cared less and less if it did. When she remembered it now and again, it was only to fret slightly over how she would write Granville Wiggins III to explain that she was no longer interested in returning east.

Then one day in the hottest part of July when Holly returned to camp, she thought she saw a stranger waiting on the porch of the cottage. The stranger stood up and walked toward the buggy. Holly's heart sank like a rock. She didn't want to believe her eyes. He was no stranger!

ten

"Holly Bennington!" The voice was breathless. The walrus-mustached man huffed down the walk toward her.

"I don't believe it!" Holly stepped down from the buggy.

Granville Wiggins III greeted her with a warm damp hand-shake and whisked off his white ten-gallon hat as he bowed. "How could I resist a letter addressed 'my dearest Granville'? At your service, ma'am."

Her head was swimming, but she managed to introduce Granville to Esmeralda and Billy Boudreau. The ever alert Esmeralda sensed Holly's consternation and excused herself immediately. Her departure was abrupt, but the significance was lost on Granville.

"Quite robust young ladies are grown out here in the wilderness." He steadied his monocle to watch the buggy roll off.

"My, what a surprise." Once alone, that was all Holly could think of to say that was truthful.

Granville wore a red neckerchief drawn tight with a turquoise-studded silver ring. His long frock coat was powder blue and piped with yellow. Long black boots almost covered the thighs of his yellow pants. She had never seen anyone dressed like Granville was now dressed in her life—except in a rainbow poster of the Wild West showman Buffalo Bill!

"Your letter was irresistible," he said.

"Where are you staying?" Holly felt years removed from Philadelphia.

"A rough gentleman by the name of Monsieur Louis Boudreau is taking care of that for me."

"He's the trader for the camp."

"A man well worth knowing then."

Her mind swirled with indecision. What was she going to say to Granville? Granville's arrival in person was much more than she had prayed for just a few weeks ago. He had come to whisk her away from this desolation. All he had to do was explain to Franklin that Holly had employment in Philadelphia. All she had to do was see that her luggage and cardboard boxes got on a freight wagon or stagecoach to Sidney, then on the train east. She was so close to leaving the wilderness. Her heart should be soaring with joy. But she felt like her breast was choked with lead. Why was she so disappointed? Why did she see Granville now as a meddling fool?

"Silent as a clam—as usual. I had forgotten." Granville's face smiled.

"I'm so surprised." Why couldn't she express herself? Was she returning to her old ways? Why was this situation so difficult for her?

"Where is Franklin?" His eyes narrowed even more than usual.

"He's on duty, getting ready for a three-day scout," she answered. "He leaves Sunday." She immediately felt lighter. She had forgotten. Franklin wasn't the sort to make a snap judgment, and he was very busy right now. He wouldn't decide tonight certainly or probably even tomorrow or possibly even the next day, Sunday. Then he would leave on the scout. Nothing could happen for three days after that. Maybe longer.

She would never ride in a freight wagon again, and she wasn't sure about the schedule of the stagecoach. Maybe the stagecoach didn't return for a week. She said cheerfully, "Let's sit on the porch."

"For you, I'll take the time. For anybody else, the business of a Wiggins is business, then more business."

Holly sat down and watched Granville try to tug some slack at the knees of his yellow pants under his enormous boots as he sat down. He carefully placed his white hat in the next chair, then arranged the lapels of his powder blue coat. Finally he laughed but not heartily enough to make his monocle pop out of his eye.

Holly studied him. He had not changed at all. He was just as she remembered him. His face was handsome with a prominent chin and strong aquiline nose. He tilted his head back so that his nostrils flared and punctuated his every sentence. His fingers groped for each other and intertwined over his red brocaded vest.

He remembered to smile again. "I see in your eyes more than gratitude for my arrival. Has something new developed?"

"That's so perceptive, Granville." This was the moment she was waiting for. She fought an overwhelming sensation of deja vu. It seemed she had this same conversation before. But of course she could not have had it before. She had never felt this way before. She must tell Granville truthfully, yet not be so tactless as to hurt him.

"It's this place. I've grown to tolerate it." Why couldn't she say she adored it? Why couldn't she say her heart lifted her out of bed every morning? Why couldn't she say she loved Red Wing and the other children? Why couldn't she admit her happiness?

"Does that mean you wish to stay?" He didn't sound annoyed.

"Perhaps a while longer." She should have felt grateful to Granville. After all, he had answered her cry for help—not with a letter, but with his considerable self. Yet he filled her with dread. Had she changed so much in one month? She did think about Jonah every day, and every day she told herself the longing for him would go away. The thought of leaving the camp and never seeing Jonah again suddenly stung her like a hornet.

"You look distressed."

"I'm thinking of the enormous inconvenience I've caused you."

He sniffed. "A gentleman must do what a gentleman must

do." He ran his fingers through coarse black hair that waved straight back. "I'll find something to do around here until you decide. My time is your time, dearest Holly." There was real joy in his voice. "After all, I wouldn't want to impose a decision on Franklin before Sunday. Then he goes away on something or other for three days. We couldn't leave yet anyway for a week, maybe two weeks."

"That's so understanding of you!" She felt like singing. "Would you like to come to the Indian village with us?"

"I don't suppose there has been any change with Bennington Brickworks, has there? Have you had any good news like you've found out the encumbrances you told me were so onerous were nothing more than trifling nuisances magnified by the hysterical imagination of a sheltered, coddled school girl?"

Holly felt her face get hot. Once in a while Granville could be painfully blunt. It wasn't intentional. She answered slowly, "No. I'm afraid there has been no change. None at all." She really hadn't even thought about Papa's brickworks for weeks. The brickworks had never been more than an abstraction to her anyway. Only their family home in Fairmont Park had been real.

"Too bad." He frowned, then took a deep breath and smiled. "Of course I'll go to the village with you."

"Wonderful." She really did feel wonderful. Granville wouldn't slow down her plans for the children at all. He might even help out.

"I'll protect you from that villain Jonah Finch!" Granville patted something under his coat.

"Villain?"

"Your letter was very specific about his underhanded activities."

"I had forgotten."

"In fact I think it imperative that you introduce me to the man. He needs to know from the outset I am now your protector. Perhaps I can even set him straight on the path to righteousness."

Granville was direct but puzzling. She shrugged it off. Why did she care if Granville was a bit puzzling? Weren't all men puzzling? She had to look at the positive aspect of Granville's surprise visit. What she first thought was a monumental nuisance would not be a nuisance at all. He wasn't terribly disturbed at the realization she might not leave with him at all. He wouldn't slow her down in the village. So she should be thankful. It was almost too good to be true.

"We have a caller!" It was Franklin voicing his pleasure as he came up the walk.

"This is Granville Wiggins III, Franklin," said Holly.

Granville stood up unsteadily in his enormous boots. "I'm honored to meet you, sir!"

Franklin's eyes were wide. "The honor is all mine. My word, Louie Boudreau warned me he had never seen a more resplendent personage. I would have to agree. Who is your outfitter, sir?"

"I'll accept your jest with my customary good nature, lieutenant. My 'outfit' as you call it was tailored by none other than Monsieur Pierre LeGrande of Chicago.

"It might be a bit hot for mid-July."

"I noticed on the stagecoach it was rather warm. But lest you think this showy dog has no bite, sir, I'll bare you these teeth!" And Granville quickly reached inside his frock coat. Metal flashed in the air.

"Look out!" Franklin jumped in front of Holly as something heavy thudded on the porch floor.

"Excuse me. My fingers were slightly cramped," said Granville. As he bent over, his monocle popped out of his eye, cutting the tension like a butter knife.

"No doubt cramped from clutching your lapels," said Holly without realizing it.

Granville picked up, then brandished, the strangest pistol Holly had ever seen. The barrel seemed stubby. Awkwardshaped handles of ivory were set in wonderfully scrolled metal. Granville said, "Colt Lightning center-fire .41. Silver-plated. A superior sidearm in every respect."

"I hope you don't plan on carrying that weapon here at the camp," said Franklin cautiously.

"Do you think it's not wise?" asked Granville.

"Definitely not."

"As you say," agreed Granville unconvincingly.

Franklin smiled at Holly. "Are you planning to show Granville about?"

She answered, "Yes, and Granville has even generously consented to go to the village with me tomorrow."

"You should have a man with you," mumbled Franklin uncharacteristically impolitic. "I'll see if Jonah is free."

Before Holly could agree, Granville blurted, "Jonah? Wonderful!"

"You don't mind?" asked Franklin with surprise.

"Of course not."

"I think I should warn you, Mr. Wiggins. If you should go out into the countryside, you would be well-advised to carry a rifle, rather than that…that revolutionary new pistol."

"Franklin! Isn't that too unkind to his nice silver pistol?" For once polite chatter was easy for Holly. She was floating. She would be with Jonah tomorrow.

Granville didn't resent Franklin's remark about his pistol at all. He was distracted by something about Franklin's uniform. "What kind of rifle do you carry, sir?"

Franklin unslung the rifle which hung from a long leather sling over his shoulder. "This is the army's standard issue for the last several years. It's called the Winchester Model .45/70."

"What do those numbers mean?" asked Granville eagerly. He had a childish look on his face as if he wanted to hear confirmation of something he knew himself.

"It shoots a .45 caliber bullet, which means the diameter of the bullet is 45 hundredths of an inch. The '70' means the cartridge has 70 grains of gunpowder. It's a very powerful, long-range shell."

"How interesting. Where do you load the bullets?"

"The shell?" Franklin popped open a metal hinge in the stock above the trigger. "This is the breech. This rifle is called a breechloader." Franklin sounded very patient. Holly suddenly realized he was explaining the rifle for her benefit, too. He continued, "This rifle will only take one shell at a time. When I pop the breech, the spent cartridge flies out."

"You hope," added Granville, and he flushed as if he wished he hadn't said it.

Franklin raised an eyebrow. "Say, you do know something of these rifles, don't you? The sad truth is that if they are fired many times in succession, the metal swells and the cartridges begin to jam."

"Yes. I believe I read it somewhere." Granville's eyes were lowered.

"Probably in the newspaper about Custer's poor unfortunate men." Franklin shook his head.

Holly didn't think so. Once again Granville was puzzling. No, she realized he was more than puzzling. He was being devious. But why should she care about a silly rifle? He wasn't pressuring her to return east. Why, she might even agree to go with him. She may have been fooling herself with this village business. Maybe she was just trying to keep her sanity.

After all, Red Wing had a good family. It wasn't as if Holly was abandoning her. And the constant Esmeralda would be there. No, she was very pleased Granville was here. She really didn't care if he wasn't being totally forthcoming. And best of all, the danger of Granville bumbling about the village would necessitate an escort. Her breast fluttered like an excited dove as she thought of Jonah. She hadn't seen him in days.

The threesome moved inside. Granville was invited to supper. Holly felt at ease to talk for once. She even had an urge to talk. She wanted to tell Granville about the camp and the village. But all through supper Granville quizzed Franklin on rifles.

"What is the rifle of preference then?" asked Granville as he finished Hop Fong's custard.

"If I could carry any rifle?" replied Franklin.

"Yes, sir, any rifle."

"I believe it would be the Model 73 Winchester."

"The repeating rifle?"

"Yes. It shoots a .44 caliber bullet with a smaller load, but I like the thought of being able to rapid fire the extra bullets. I would sacrifice the extra range for the extra bullets. Hostile Indians have a nasty habit of getting quite close to their enemies, so the extra range is of little use."

"And is this the general opinion of you Westerners?"

"Yes, I believe so."

"Would a savage be able to operate such a weapon?"

"Yes, unfortunately, very easily. And I can certainly understand why you are so concerned."

Granville seemed strangely relieved. He became ebullient. "My compliments to Mr. Hop Fong for his most excellent Cantonese egg rolls. It's not my preferred Chinese cuisine, but it was quite tasty. Personally I prefer spicy Szechwan cooking, too hot for most people—certainly too hot for the little ladies."

"I'll ask Hop Fong if he can cook a meal to your taste, Mr. Wiggins," said Franklin agreeably.

"In fact," shouted Granville, "if I'm not mistaken Mr. Hop Fong has in stock some fagara spice known to lesser gourmets as Szechwan pepper." Granville lurched toward the cast-iron stove and picked up a large shaker. "Yes, I believe this is it." He sprinkled some powder on his palm. "Just the thing!" He flipped the spice cavalierly into his mouth. He slammed the shaker down on the stove. His monocle popped from his eye.

Franklin jumped up. "Are you all right?"

"Of course," replied Granville in a thin voice. His eyes were teary. He picked up his glass and gulped water so fast that it dribbled off his chin. He slammed the glass down on the table."Well, I've enjoyed the hospitality, but I really must be turning in." His voice was as thin as a thread. "I assume we will start early tomorrow morning. Everyone out here seems to rise before the rooster." His voice was nearly gone.

After Granville hastily left, Franklin seemed lost in thought. Finally he turned to Holly. "I'm going to be very busy getting ready for the scout, and I leave Sunday. Keep a watchful eye on your friend."

"What do you suspect?"

"Suspect! Why, I only meant for you to watch out for a green-horn. My word, did you see the way the peacock fumbled that pistol about? Although I guess I shouldn't blame him. Poor balance is a chief fault of the pistol, in addition to being very inaccurate because of the stubby barrel and the heavy trigger pull of a double-action. Not to mention he'll find no one selling .41 center-fire bullets within a hundred miles."

"What does 'double action' mean?"

"It means you don't have to cock the hammer before it will fire. You just pull the trigger. In the case of Granville Wiggins III, that convenience is to the distinct disadvantage of the rest of mankind."

"I've never known you to be so critical." And she added *even unkind* in her thoughts. She realized she felt strongly about Granville. Yes, he was a peacock. But hadn't she strutted into the wilderness with a chip on her shoulder, too?

"He will bear watching. You haven't seen the serious side of the Lakotas I've seen. They won't tolerate a fool."

She wanted to change the subject. In her small way she would defend Granville. "You won't tell me your experiences with the Lakotas. Esmeralda told me you were at the Battle of the Rosebud. Were you?"

"Yes." He smiled. "I forget how much you know now. I love you like a little sister, but I know I must stop thinking you know only as much as a little sister. Esmeralda tells me that you're the best help she's had since she started working in the village."

"No!" Holly was stunned. Oh, sweet Esmeralda. How could she have caused Esmeralda trouble? Holly tried to compose herself. Praise was so unsettling. "Let's not talk about me. Tell me about the Rosebud."

"Crazy Horse attacked us near the deep canyon of the Rosebud River. We had over a thousand soldiers in the 2nd and 3rd Cavalry and two regiments of Infantry. We were on the way to the huge Lakota village on the Little Big Horn that Custer's Seventh Cavalry found a few days later only 25 miles northwest of where we were. I rode in Company A naturally. Our general sent Company A and seven other companies into the canyon of the Rosebud to go on through and find the village."

Franklin stopped. His voice was choked. "Over 400 of us. More soldiers than Custer lost. The canyon was a trap. Crazy Horse attacked the general and the other troops that didn't go down the canyon so furiously that our general had to call us back. That's the only thing that saved us. Crazy Horse was going to trap us in the canyon right after he surrounded the general. We were nearly all doomed—as doomed as Custer." He held his thumb and index finger a hair apart. "We came that close to dying that day."

"But don't you think God saved you?"

"God's will was done."

"God 'sends rain on the righteous and the unrighteous,' Matthew chapter 5, verse 45."

"Like I said," laughed Franklin easily. "I keep forgetting how much you know now. Yes, I like that passage because Crazy Horse is like some immense force of nature."

"What was the outcome of the battle?"

"When Crazy Horse saw that we didn't fall into the trap and we pulled back to concentrate our forces, he tried to pull us apart with small skirmishes all day. Very few warriors and soldiers were killed. But he succeeded in stopping us. We no longer pushed on to the great Lakota village to the northwest but waited like a fat exhausted hog for more supplies. So, in a way, Custer was doomed that day at the Rosebud."

"It all seems so awful. Why do you do it?"

"We are peacemakers, Holly. I know we don't look like it, but we are. There is a relentless flood of whites coming into this prairie—some as evil as any men who ever walked the earth and some as innocent as babies—and we must be the peacemakers."

Franklin was in such a wistful, compliant mood that Holly could not resist asking, "And where was peacemaker Jonah Finch during the battle?"

"Jonah? Why do you ask about Jonah? He's a civilian."

"Since when?"

Franklin studied her. "I guess you found out he went to West Point. Many cadets resign their commissions."

"But did Jonah?"

"Well, you see for yourself he doesn't wear a uniform."

"You're ducking every question now. You always were an unenthusiastic liar, Franklin. I won't embarrass you and force you to lie. For some reason, you and the army still protect Jonah. Someday soon I'll discover Jonah's terrible secret."

And she told herself as she went to sleep that night that there was no better time than tomorrow.

eleven

The next morning Jonah Finch's huge bay kept pace on the driver's side of the buggy in an easy smooth walk. The reddish-brown coat was groomed to a high gloss. It was the first time Holly had seen Jonah ride his bay. He sat astride a lightweight military saddle with no saddle horn. He sat tall with the small of his back arched slightly forward. He held the reins lightly in front of the saddle. His wide shoulders scarcely moved. The bay seemed to guide itself. Jonah rode very well. He whistled softly.

Holly hadn't seen Jonah that much lately. She tried to burn his image in her mind. He wore his usual garb of wide-brimmed tan hat, white cotton shirt, buckskin pants, and rawhide boots. For a while he took off his hat and let the breeze riff his hair. She wouldn't forget one strand of his sunny red hair. It was a very pleasant task. It would have been a tranquil trip except for Granville.

"So what kind of weaponry would you recommend in the wilderness, Mr. Finch?" yelled Granville.

Jonah stopped whistling in the middle of "The Daring Young Man on the Flying Trapeze."

"Depends on what game you are hunting, Mr. Wiggins."

"Hunting? I don't mean hunting. I meant weaponry for protection—against the savages."

Jonah frowned. "You aren't carrying a weapon now, are you, Mr. Wiggins?"

"No sir. I left my double-action Colt Lightning with Monsieur Louis Boudreau."

"That's good," said Jonah. "Well, Mr. Wiggins, I would say in your case your best weapon against savages would be to

103

extend your right index finger, touch your nose with it, then touch the left side of your chest with it, then throw your hand straight forward." Jonah made the signs as he described them.

"What is that mumbo jumbo?" Granville's jaw dropped. He looked at Esmeralda, who had her head turned away but seemed to be smiling. Granville looked at Holly for the first time since they left the camp. "Is he joking?"

"I don't think so," answered Holly. "He thinks your best chance for survival is to greet the so-called savages as if you're very happy to see them."

"Sign language? Does he think I'm a mute?" grumbled Granville. He shouted, "But what kind of weapon would you use against the attacking red horde, Mr. Finch?"

"I'm civilian, Mr. Wiggins, as in 'civil.'"

"Quite an agrarian wit," muttered Granville.

Lakota women and children were waiting for them at the trader's building in the village. The women already fed pine logs to a quick hot fire. Several raised blankets across their faces when they noticed Granville.

"We're making soap today, Granville," explained Holly.

Granville's nostrils had never been higher. "No doubt there is a crying need for it, but strangely I don't smell anything malodorous," he answered. He carefully folded his powder blue frock coat and placed it in the buggy.

Esmeralda had been silent the entire trip. But she seemed very amused with Granville, ever since she first saw his white ten-gallon hat. "Mr. Wiggins," she entreated.

"Please! Call me Granville." He eagerly bowed. "At your service, Miss Monroe."

"You will serve? How kind. Would you mind carrying to the fire that kettle of beef fat that is hanging over there on that tripod?"

"Me?" Granville's monocle darted around like a chameleon's eye. "Where is Mr. Finch? Has he disappeared? He's as quiet as a cat when he's not whistling."

"I'm sure he's taking care of the horses." Esmeralda smiled sweetly at Granville.

Holly saw that Jonah already had the saddle off his bay and was rubbing grass over his back.

"How long will that peculiar ritual take?" asked Granville.

Esmeralda answered, "Why, as long as it takes to cool off, water, and feed two very valuable animals."

"So he's going to unhitch your horse from the buggy and do all that rigmarole to it, too?" grunted Granville. Some of the Lakota children were frowning at him. "What's wrong with them?"

"They don't know the strange ways of Philadelphia, Granville," answered Holly. "Out here every man takes care of his horse before himself."

"Of course. I should have known," muttered Granville. His enormous boots raised dust as he walked toward the kettle on the tripod. "Is there some beef fat under all those flies?" he asked, not expecting an answer. He waved his arm and a cloud of flies exploded into the air. "There. I made the kettle ten pounds lighter."

He lugged the kettle to the fire. Unfortunately, by the time he set the kettle down, his long black boots and nice yellow pants were smeared with grease and soot.

"Thank you," said Esmeralda. "Now could you please shovel some lye from that trough into this kettle?" She smiled as she pointed to another kettle and added, "Granville."

"At your service, Miss Monroe."

Every few seconds Granville checked on Jonah. He seemed more and more exasperated as Jonah rubbed down the second horse with grass, then curried both horses, then covered them with a blanket before walking them. Finally Jonah watered each horse and fed them some oats from a bag in the back of the buggy. Then he tethered them in the shade of the trader's building. He patted them both affectionately and walked inside the trader's building.

Granville leaned on the shovel and grumbled, "I thought horses were supposed to do the work."

By the time the kettle of lye was boiling over the fire and Esmeralda was carefully adding pieces of beef fat from the other kettle, Granville looked like he might have to use all the soap they could make on himself and his clothes.

"Excuse me, ladies," he grunted after he took a good look at his clothes. He walked inside the trader's building. When he came out fifteen minutes later he carried his long boots and a folded stack of clothes. He was wearing rawhide boots, blue denim pants, and a blue cotton shirt. "Cleaner but not wiser. What do I do next, Miss Monroe?" he said to Esmeralda. He may have tried to wink at her because his monocle suddenly popped out.

Holly was surprised. Although Granville hated the work they were doing, he continued to help anyway. His grumbling seemed to amuse Esmeralda as much as Holly. Even the Lakotas became amused with his good-humored griping and lack of aptitude for work. Somehow Jonah had disappeared. That was his way; he came and went as quietly and inexplicably as a cat.

By noon Jonah returned. Holly and Esmeralda were ladling off soap floating on the top of the boiling kettle and dropping it into a third kettle of unheated water. Eventually the soap would harden.

Granville grinned at Jonah. "At last you're back, Mr. Finch. Do you suppose you could show me what the men do around here? I mean in the Indian village."

"Ladies," said Jonah, very seriously, "I believe the heavy part is done. I'm sure you won't mind if I show Mr. Wiggins around."

Granville looked like a man just acquitted of a crime. His voice was pure joy. "If the ladies don't mind, I would be delighted, Mr. Finch."

The two men disappeared into the sea of tepees. They were nearly the same height. *Why*, thought Holly, *did Jonah seem so much taller?* But she had changed her mind about Granville. He was a stuffed shirt, but he was a humorous stuffed shirt. And he seemed able to take ribbing and even make fun of himself. So maybe it was just his refined Philadelphia mannerisms. But she was from Philadelphia. So was Franklin. Did they appear to be as snooty as Granville? Maybe she could love Granville.

"How many kinds of love are there?" she said without thinking she said it aloud.

Esmeralda stood up from the kettle. She looked in the direction Jonah and Granville walked. With mischief in her eyes she quoted:

> "How do I love thee? Let me count the ways.
> I love thee to the depth and breadth and height
> My soul can reach, when feeling out of sight
> for the ends of Being and Ideal Grace."

Holly quoted the next lines of the sonnet:

> "I love thee to the level of every day's
> Most quiet need, by sun and candlelight.
> I love thee freely, as man strive for Right;
> I love thee purely, as they turn from Praise;
> I love thee with the passion put to use
> In my old Griefs, and with my childhood's faith."

Esmeralda continued, staring in the direction of the camp:

> "I love thee with a love I seemed to lose
> With my lost saints—I love thee with the breath,
> Smiles, tears, of all my life!—and, if God choose,
> I shall but love thee better after death."

"Wonderful!" Holly clapped her hands together in joy. But

her joy evaporated. "Do only poets like Elizabeth Barrett Browning know what love is?" she murmured. "Surely not."

"'Love the Lord your God with all your heart and with all your soul and with all your mind.'"

Holly added, "And the second commandment is, 'Love your neighbor as yourself.'"

"Matthew, chapter 23."

Holly felt dizzy. "We are so much alike, Esmeralda."

"Yes. I too ponder the kinds of love."

"All real love comes from God's love."

"Surely. And we love God.

"And a woman loves a man. But surely that's not the same kind of love I feel for God. And love of God and love of a man can't be the same as my love for Red Wing. And I don't think my love for Red Wing is exactly the same as love for a neighbor."

"Or Jonah's love of animals."

"Or love for a place. It's so complicated," sighed Holly.

"God makes life complicated and mysterious. Not to confuse us, but to enrich us. How wonderful it is that we have so many kinds of love." Esmeralda laughed. "Besides, you are not so much concerned with the kinds of love but with who loves whom."

"Not at all. But just out of curiosity, how would you choose a man?"

"I'm not sure if a choice is always available, but I would choose the man on the straightest path."

All afternoon Holly thought about love. Could she ever love a man like Granville? She liked him more now than she ever did before. Sure, he was dressed foolishly, but how was a Philadelphian to know what they wore in the wilderness? What a sacrifice he had made to come all this way after her. If he were being ridiculed, it was only because of her. How could she repay him? Could she learn to love a man like Granville? She had no reason to think he was not on the straight path. But then what did she really know about him?

And what about Jonah? Her heart fluttered when he was around her, even now when he was only in her thoughts. But he carried some awful secret. He really was on a crooked path of some kind. She was sure of that. But no. Perhaps he had repented. Perhaps he had changed to a straight path. Could she ever love a man like Jonah? Could she love him if she later found she couldn't respect him? What terrible thing might be revealed about him next week, next month, next year?

She remembered how she had tried to create mischief between Esmeralda and Jonah. How could she have done that to her own brother Franklin? Or sweet Esmeralda? Holly really had grown in the last few weeks. Why? Was it the demands of the wilderness? Was it the sweet influence of Esmeralda? Was it the strength of Jonah or patience of Franklin? Or was it Christ? After all, she was soaking up God's Word in a way she hadn't in years.

Holly couldn't sort it all out. But she felt intense gratitude for finding her way back to Scripture. She wanted to cry tears of joy. She felt Red Wing clinging by her side. Red Wing's eyes were bright with worry. The small girl's forehead was creased with lines that should not be there.

Red Wing held her fingers to her heart and signed as if she were throwing her heart to the ground. She pointed to Holly. "Why sad?" she struggled to say.

Holly grabbed her and hugged her. "Oh you little dear, Red Wing! I love you!"

Jonah and Granville returned in the late afternoon. They were on a first name basis.

Jonah said, "Look, Granville. The ladies are making fine soap."

Granville said, "Still making soap soup? I can see not much has happened here since I left, Jonah."

Holly and Esmeralda laughed, so rudely that even Jonah's face registered surprise. He smiled a question. "I would love to know what else happened here."

"Nothing compared to what we did, I'm sure," said Granville. "Ladies, I met some Lakota warriors, fine strapping young lads. I'm going to work with them. I mean I'm going to work with Jonah when he works with them. They are a bit rough around the edges. They played a game with me I don't care to make part of my daily routine."

"The young warriors love to test newcomers with the 'eyelash game'," explained Jonah. Jonah's face showed he was genuinely impressed with Granville. "They got right in Granville's face and plucked several of his eyelashes to see if he would flinch." Jonah winced as he said it. "He passed with flying colors. I've rarely seen someone so determined."

"Granville, I'm so proud of you," said Holly. She was amazed. The Lakota men wouldn't tolerate a fool, yet Granville had passed the test with flying colors!

Granville shrugged. "Well, let's hope the young warriors got their fill of that childish and excruciatingly painful game. I would sooner look forward to a life of toothaches and hang-nails."

Jonah said, "We are going to show the young warriors how to take care of cattle. And sheep, too, Miss Monroe." He tipped his hat to Esmeralda. "Of course they love their horses and dogs, but they have never kept animals for food and hides. The buffalo was all they needed. They love the buffalo."

"The eyelash test wasn't our only experience this afternoon," Granville added. "I also met Chief Crazy Horse. I even talked to him. He didn't exactly talk back to me. Speechless I guess."

Holly and Esmeralda laughed again.

"The chief sticks two measly hawk feathers in his hair," grumbled Granville. "If I were invincible in battle like he is, I would wear a couple of hundred eagle feathers draping off a headdress of enormous buffalo horns."

Holly and Esmeralda laughed again.

Granville had a worried expression. "You ladies are giddy.

You have been bending over those soap fumes too long. Perhaps I should take you back to the camp."

"Shall I hitch up the horse, Esmeralda?" asked Jonah innocently.

Holly noticed Jonah seemed as amused by Granville as she and Esmeralda were. Suddenly she appreciated Jonah even more. What if he had treated Granville badly? She knew how some people mindlessly resented newcomers. Some of the young ladies at Gladwyne never accepted her, never even talked to her once, never even gave her the slightest chance. But not Jonah. Jonah treated Granville almost like a brother.

Esmeralda said, "I agree with Mr. Wiggins. It has been a long hot day by these kettles."

"Come on. Let's hitch up the horse, Granville," said Jonah. And amazingly he threw his arm around Granville's shoulder and the two men walked toward the trader's building where Jonah had tethered the horses.

Now Holly was really puzzled. The two men walked a perfectly straight path. But who was guiding whom?

Several minutes later Jonah, mounted on his bay, rode beside the westbound buggy. Holly sat between Esmeralda and Granville, who worked constantly with the reins. Holly knew such attention was unnecessary; the horse remembered the way back to camp better than they did.

And it was on the way back to camp that Holly had another revelation in a day brimming with revelations.

twelve

Holly could see the legs of Jonah's big bay swing in an easy trot beside Esmeralda. Jonah was hidden from Holly by the hood over the buggy. If she leaned forward she could see his knees and boots. The conversation between Jonah and Esmeralda was innocent enough. They talked of Deadwood and other places in the wilderness that were no more than homely names to Holly.

Once she did lean forward and ask Jonah, "And how did Cat Head Creek get its name?"

"What?" he asked.

Holly looked at Esmeralda. "What did Jonah say? I couldn't hear him.'

"He said, 'What?'"

"Oh, never mind."

Holly realized she would have to yell to communicate with Jonah, and she couldn't bring herself to do such an unladylike thing. There was nothing worse than a lady yelling like a banshee. She patted Esmeralda's arm like she really didn't mind. But she felt more and more isolated in the middle of the seat. And it was worst when they laughed in the pleasure of each other's company.

Why didn't Jonah just sit tall on his bay and whistle like he usually did? Why did he have to talk to Esmeralda? All the sober things he was saying to Esmeralda should have been said to Holly. Why didn't he just bolt off and ride on to the camp?

"Nothing bad can happen to us now," she muttered.

"What, dear?" Esmeralda looked at her with kind eyes.

"Oh, nothing."

Holly felt her anger grow. Or was it jealousy? How could she feel jealous of sweet Esmeralda? But the hot black feeling grew. Her hands trembled. She clasped them together and held them close. Holly felt like crying. Jonah might be so wrong for her. But she felt so strongly about him. How would she ever overcome this deep inner feeling? Was it love? Was she fighting love?

Esmeralda touched her arm and whispered, "Holly, my dear, you're crying."

"I accidentally looked into the sun for a moment," she explained and tried to smile. She quickly added, "The rays are vicious this time of day." Tacking a truth onto her lie made it seem less bad.

All the while the buggy clattered along, Granville talked. He rarely ever asked her a question, so she didn't have to listen. She sneaked a peek. Yes, he had his head tilted back, his nostrils flaring as he talked to the bobbing horse head more than her. But Holly was glad he was so preoccupied with his own conversation. He didn't notice she was crying. He wouldn't blurt out the fact that she was crying. Jonah mustn't know. She was glad now he couldn't see her. She didn't want to appear so weak. She didn't want to blubber a weak explanation. Would the ride to camp ever end?

Oh, why did everything come back to Jonah? He might be so wrong. The ache she felt must be love. How could her heart be so out of harmony with the truth?

When the buggy stopped in front of the cottage, she blurted, "Excuse me. I'm not feeling well." She quickly slipped past Esmeralda and jumped down right past Jonah's outstretched hands. She hiked up the front of her skirt, feeling hot and foolish, and hurried inside.

She felt much better inside. She leaned her back against the door and thanked God she could be alone with her feelings which were flooding to the surface. Her mind was swimming with contradictions. Why was she so strongly attracted to Jonah?

He might be so wrong for her. Esmeralda was surely right. Choose a man on a straight path. How could any God-fearing woman do otherwise?

And yet every fiber of her being told her Granville might be wrong for her, too. And he was on the straight path. How could Holly's affection be so turned around? And why was life in this world such a cruel joke? She thanked God tomorrow was Sunday. No one would go to the village to work anyway. Dear little Red Wing would not expect her. She would tell Franklin she was sick and wanted no callers. No. She couldn't do that. She had to go to church with Franklin after the camp had its Sunday morning inspection. Then she would get sick. She mustn't forget to get sick right after church. Being devious was so demanding. There was so much to remember.

But she had time now to think it out. She sat down in a chair in the living room. Franklin would be leaving on the scout Sunday afternoon. She would be free to relax and really think things out. And if she hadn't sorted things out by Monday morning she would stay 'sick.' Her plan was quite good. And innocent enough. Surely it was all right to do what she was doing. But somehow she felt queasy about it.

"You're home?" It was Franklin. He had been in the study. Why hadn't she noticed the closed door?

"Yes. Resting. It was hot today." More half-truths. Why was she so sly?

"I thought you were reading the Scriptures again."

The Bible was on the table beside her chair. "No, I wasn't," she answered too defensively. Why was she so snippy? Was it because the Bible would make her feel guilty about her plans?

"Dear Holly," said Franklin, "you work so hard in the village."

They barely spoke after that. Franklin was obviously engrossed in his plans for the scout. And Holly did not want to talk. Her emotions were too close to the surface today for some reason. If Franklin even mentioned Jonah's name, she probably would burst into tears. What was happening to her?

That night she prayed for God's will to be done. It was hard for her to find sleep. She kept thinking about Jonah and fighting the thought with all her heart and soul that God was betraying her. Yet, that question kept slithering into her mind to haunt her. Why would He abandon her to such a man as Jonah?

Franklin's first words at breakfast were, "You look very tired. Are you sick?"

"I don't feel well. It's true." It was true. And she felt some satisfaction from that. It would make her plan even more believable. Surely now before he left on the scout Franklin would tell Esmeralda, Poor Holly isn't feeling well. And Esmeralda would reply, Yes, poor Holly looked like she was getting sick yesterday. Holly smiled and, startled by it, quickly glanced at Franklin. He hadn't noticed her satisfied little smile; all his concentration was focused on Hop Fong's scrambled eggs.

She and Franklin rode in a buggy unfamiliar to Holly. Church was held in the open air close to the laundry building on the shore of a creek. It was an area spacious enough for a thousand men. One thousand men also generated an astonishing amount of laundry. Out of the corner of her eye, Holly saw hundreds of shirts and pants and sheets flagging in the brisk wind. That sight and its flapping sound were pleasant. Order was reassuring. The chaplain's sermon was excellent. Two men were baptized in the creek. She really felt close to God. In fact, she felt wonderful. She had to remember not to look perky.

But why didn't she abandon her plan? What was the point now? She felt confident. Suddenly she saw a red-haired man way off to the side, hands folded, head down. He had a neckerchief pulled high around his face. He kept his head down. Was it Jonah? He stood so tall. He looked so sturdy. He was so reverent. She really hoped it was Jonah. Yes, she would truly love to see Jonah worshipping God. Of course, that would answer her prayer. Surely it was Jonah. She could abandon her plan.

The redhead glanced up.

He was not Jonah!

Tears welled in Holly's eyes. Her upper lip quivered. She was an emotional custard, ready to quiver to the slightest vibration. She certainly couldn't give up her plan now. She wouldn't be able to see anyone for days and days and days. She couldn't remember a time when her feelings were so fragile.

After the service, Franklin drove the buggy east toward the stables. He should have turned north before he reached them. But he didn't. Holly protested, "I'm not feeling well. Could you please take me back to the cottage?"

"I'm very sorry, but I have to take care of some things here. I won't see you again until after the three-day scout. But I know you're in good hands with Esmeralda."

"But how do I get back to the cottage?" This complication made her almost forget her big problem.

"Jonah will take you."

"Jonah!" How could Franklin do this to her? She sputtered, "C...c...can't you take me?"

"There he is." Franklin waved. "Over here, Jonah!"

And Jonah walked toward the buggy, carrying a rifle. "Morning, folks."

Holly said nothing more than a cool good-bye to Franklin. Jonah slipped the rifle under the seat and climbed up into the buggy. He didn't seem any more inclined to talk than Holly. She was counting the seconds until Jonah stopped the buggy in front of the cottage where she could leap out and run inside. He headed the buggy west and then north past the laundry building. Good. Holly saw the post commander's house. In seconds Jonah would turn east and stop in front of the cottage. There she would escape before her feelings bubbled to the surface. She didn't even know what her feelings would be. Anger? Jealousy? Love?

But Jonah didn't turn east. "You're driving north!" she cried. "Where do you think you are going?"

"Why, I thought you'd like a ride toward the bluffs. Everyone drives about the countryside on Sunday mornings."

"Why didn't you go to church?" she blurted.

He blinked in surprise. "I apologize. I know I should have."

"What is your excuse, sir?"

"I have one. But I would rather not say what it is."

She wanted to shout, Liar! but realized she had been telling lies herself lately. Of course she had good reason. Nevertheless she didn't feel like scolding him. There was a more immediate problem.

"I do not wish to go into the countryside with you."

He reined in the horse and threw the hand brake. "Of course, ma'am." He took off his wide-brimmed tan hat. He raised the hood of the buggy over their heads. "Best keep the summer sun off that fair skin of yours." His eyes swept over her. Her heart twittered like a small appreciative bird and that made her very angry.

"I can't believe your impertinence."

"I noticed how stirred up you were yesterday. I had to talk to you."

She felt very angry. Why did Jonah have to talk to her? Was Franklin countering her earlier schemes with a scheme of his own? Was he now cynically promoting some relationship between Holly and Jonah? Was Jonah's friendliness just encouraged by Franklin so Holly would ease off her scheme with Esmeralda and Jonah? Such scheming didn't seem like something Franklin would do, but Holly was angry at being trapped with Jonah.

"Did Franklin put you up to this?" she snapped.

"He's concerned about you. So am I." He touched her hand.

"Please, sir!" His large thick hand withdraw. It was tan with freckles. She searched his face. His skin was reddish gold, probably as dark as it could ever get. His eyes were serene but very concerned. Suddenly she wanted to throw her arms around his neck and hug him. Why did he make her feel so affectionate? Why had she swung suddenly from anger to affection? She trembled.

He said, "I like you very much, Holly. I can't look at you without wanting to hug you. I don't know why you make me feel such affection..."

Why, those were her very same thoughts! She gasped. It was time for the truth. She said softly, "I like you too." *Like* sounded so pitifully inadequate. "But you are so mysterious. You frighten me."

"I'm afraid you'll have to trust me. I'm not so mysterious. In fact I'd like to be very truthful with you always. I mean truthful regarding my feelings. I've never had that freedom with anyone."

"I did. Once."

"With your mother?"

"How did you know?"

"Franklin told me."

"How is it you two are such friends?"

"Who can explain friendship but God? Who can explain the friendship between Jonathan and David? Or...you and me." He touched her hand. This time she didn't withdraw.

"Is that what it is? Friendship?"

"We best call it that for now."

For now? she thought. *And what was later?*

The buggy was spinning. She felt short of breath. She tilted her head back and closed her eyes. If only a breeze would cool her face. She felt dizzy. Soft warmth smothered her lips. No. It couldn't be. No man had ever done that to her. Was this her first kiss? She opened her eyes. Yes, he was kissing her! Her head was swimming. She felt like she was melting. She wanted him to hold her. She would do anything to keep that moment. She pulled away from him. Or had he pulled away from her? She didn't know. She had never felt so dizzy. No, it was giddy. No, it was ecstasy. Rapture. At last she knew real passion. She was afraid to open her eyes. What would she say now?

He said, "That was wonderful, Holly. You are as sweet as I

thought you would be. But we best move on."

He drove the buggy toward the bluffs. She tried to clear her thoughts. Her head swarmed with a million reasons to go and a million reasons to stop. "Where are you going?" she asked breathlessly.

"Oh, I'll stop by the bluffs. If we stay here, every Sunday stroller from the camp will pass by and gawk."

"Oh." Her heart was soaring. She had never noticed before how soft and supple the prairie grass seemed. And the yucca had stems covered with creamy blossoms.

He finally did stop the buggy. The bluffs were close. Holly had a feeling of dread. Why? Now the grass was bristly and the yucca prickly. Dark canyons sliced back in the bluffs.

Men rode from the nearest canyon!

"Stay calm," said Jonah.

Ten men approached. They were Lakota!

They formed a semicircle ahead of the buggy. One Lakota slipped off his horse. He wore blue denims and a leather vest. On his head was a small war bonnet with eagle feathers. He strutted toward Jonah.

Jonah held his hand up in front palm down, then swept his hand to the right side turning thumb up. "No! This is no time for talk."

"No talk, Finch!" barked the brave on foot. And he thrust his fist forward with the thumb between the index and middle finger. "I look now!"

"You've looked, kola. Now move on."

"Look at gun." The brave pointed under the seat of the buggy.

Jonah sighed and reached under the seat. He held up the rifle. "Here. Take a good look."

The brave's hand was lightning. He yanked the rifle from Jonah's hands. "I try it." And he pulled the rifle to his shoulder and pointed it around the countryside. He made booming sounds like a child. "Winchester—repeating."

"Yes."

Winchester Model 73, thought Holly. *The repeating rifle Franklin said was his favorite.*

The brave pointed the rifle toward the bluffs. Even to Holly it was a beautiful rifle. The sleek stock was dark oiled hardwood of some kind. The metal was blue-black and looked as sturdy as granite.

Suddenly the rifle exploded. The brave pumped a lever under the trigger and the rifle exploded again. In the bluffs dust flew into the air. Holly noticed how Jonah was clenching his jaw each time the rifle exploded. And the brave fired it twelve times!

Finally the brave lowered the rifle. "How many, Finch?" He was smiling as he handed the rifle back to Jonah.

Jonah held up five fingers and said nothing. He took the rifle back angrily and stowed it under the seat.

Holly realized the brave was looking at her now. He walked around the buggy, stopped and put his hands on his hips. "Who squaw, Finch?"

"My squaw."

"Look at hands?" The brave pointed at Holly.

She held out one hand. The brave roughly grabbed it and turned it over. His jaw dropped. "Pretty squaw work plenty much too, Finch?"

"For me." Jonah slapped his chest.

"Maybe squaw work for Bloody Hawk, Finch." He pounded his chest.

"No!" Jonah's face was red. And he thrust his fist forward with the thumb between the index and middle finger. He angrily barked, "Go!"

"Okay, Finch." The brave hurled himself on his horse and the ten riders thundered back into the canyon.

Holly scarcely knew where to start with her questions. She started with a complaint. "Am I your squaw now?"

"I'm sorry. I had to say that. He was getting too interested in you."

"Oh."

Jonah rubbed his hand through his hair. He was upset. "The post commander is going to be very unhappy about those gunshots."

"You can start by explaining them to me."

"What is there to explain? Some braves were out riding around, which they do all the time to make sure white skunks aren't stealing their horses, and they wanted to look at my rifle."

"Bloody Hawk?"

"What did you say?

"That brave said he was Bloody Hawk."

"You misunderstood. His name was Muddy Haunch."

"But I...." Holly fell into silence. *Oh please, God, don't let it all turn bad.* Surely Jonah couldn't be a gunrunner. But the brave whatever he was called seemed to know Jonah very well. In spite of their angry exchanges Jonah even called him kola, the Lakota word for friend. And the brave seemed to expect to see the rifle. And she was sure he said his name was Bloody Hawk...

Oh God, please make me wrong, she prayed. How could she love Jonah if she wasn't wrong about all that?

thirteen

The day was hot now. The sun hurt her eyes. And the truth ached inside her.

"Are you all right?" asked Jonah.

"Maybe I shouldn't see you for a few days."

"I'm afraid I can't honor your request. I promised Franklin would go with you and Esmeralda to the village."

"Only because of Granville Wiggins III."

"Yes. That's true."

"So why don't you go to the village separately with Granville He's not working with us anyway. Billy Boudreau can take u to the village like he always does."

"All right." Jonah's eyes were disappointed. He waved cor dially at officers and their ladies as they passed. But he re mained silent all the way back to the cottage. His good-by was somber.

Holly spent the rest of Sunday praying and thinking. Dee in her heart her love for Jonah seemed pure and blessed. Bu her head told her there was more between Jonah and the te Lakota warriors than an accidental meeting. And it explaine why Jonah's presence at the camp seemed so pointless. He wa a gunrunner.

Who could she turn to?

For the first time in many days, she remembered what Blabb had told her at the station between Sidney and Camp Robinso There was an Army officer looking into the nasty business gunrunning. That officer was Franklin!

How could she have forgotten? But she couldn't tell Frankli her concerns yet. Franklin was on a scout. Could she te Esmeralda? No, she decided. She must be patient. She woul go to the village and act as normal as possible. In fact she would move beyond normal; it was time she pushed ahead with her idea about educating the Lakota children. She was not going to allow herself to become befuddled over some criminal scheme like gunrunning and make the Lakota children suffer.

The next morning she strode to the buggy more determined than ever.

"Are you feeling better?" were Esmeralda's first words. Her square face was marred by worry.

"Yes. I'm fine today." Holly remembered her deception. How unexpectedly such lies sprang back to life.

"Franklin's last words to me were, 'Poor Holly isn't feeling well,' so I was worried about you yesterday. I would have called on you, but I know when I don't feel well the last thing I want is the company of someone in high spirits."

"How considerate of you. Yes, yesterday I was out of sorts. I wasn't sick exactly." There. Holly was undoing the lie. She would tell the truth, some of it anyway. "I started the day with the blues. After church I felt better. Then I fell under the spell again. I spent the whole rest of the day in intense contemplation. Finally I recovered and now I feel quite optimistic."

"My! May I ask the nature of your blues?"

"Oh, it was just from growing pains." Holly felt a twinge of guilt. Her answer was so evasive. "But I will gladly tell you the nature of my recovery. It involves my work in the village."

"Do you not want to help us harvest leeks today?"

"Oh, I do. I was looking forward to the soup we are going to make with leeks and beef. But I want to begin teaching the children to speak and write English."

Esmeralda put her hand to her face. "Oh, you must talk to the Indian Agent first." She put her hand down and composed herself. "What I mean is that I, too, once had that idea. And the Indian Agent squelched it. He thought the Lakota were less likely to cause mischief if they didn't know English."

"But surely you didn't discuss it with the new agent Mr. Irwin. He only just got here."

Esmeralda's face became radiant. "You see how important it is to get new blood in the camp! I was so burned by my bad failure I had given up trying again. I would have thought of trying again eventually, I suppose."

Holly suddenly realized that her dream had once been Esmeralda's dream. And who deserved more to realize their dream? She said, "You must go to the agent, Esmeralda. If you want me to help I will. But you had the idea first."

"No. You go. I promised the women I would harvest leeks with them today. And that is what I am going to do."

"That's very important, too. We must help the Lakota supplement their meat diet." Holly tried very hard to make Esmeralda's work sound as important as educating the children.

"Corn would be ideal. But they are not ready for that. Too many of their old enemies are corn growers. It will be many years before they will be willing to plant corn. In the meantime we must get them to raise hardy vegetables." Esmeralda laughed. "I sound like I'm trying to convince you. And it's you who should be rehearsing, so you can convince the new Indian Agent that English would be a good thing for the Lakotas."

"Oh, Esmeralda, everything is so political. What should I say to him?"

"Assure him you won't preach to them. Assure him it will make his job easier. Assure him it will reflect well on him with his superiors. Assure him you seek no glory for yourself and you will remain virtually invisible."

"All that?"

"And that may not be enough. It wasn't enough for the old agent."

Holly wanted to hug Esmeralda. She had been through so much, and yet she never spoke of her trials, unless asked.

Uneasily, Holly admitted to herself that she had been naive. She'd thought she would set up a trestle supporting some kind of painted board she could chalk lessons on and gradually get more and more Lakota children to come and learn English. If she could make it entertaining enough for them, she was sure it would work. After all, the children were with the mothers and grandmothers. And more and more of the mothers and grandmothers flocked to Esmeralda every day.

But now she had to convince the Indian Agent. She remembered the good advice Esmeralda told her. And she prayed, *God's will be done.*

Agent Irwin saw Holly immediately. He was sitting at his desk in the small agency office behind a sea of paper.

"Come in," he said, with a trace of exasperation. Holly was one more unexpected thing he had to deal with in a day choked with problems. Holly had heard him complaining. Beef shipments were late. Flour was spoiled. Lakota horses were being stolen. Warriors were being sold whiskey. The problems were without end.

Holly tensed her muscles as hard as she could. She relaxed them and took a deep breath. "I would like to help you with something, Mr. Irwin. The Lakota children are restless. Restless children cause trouble."

"Yes." He watched her suspiciously. Was he thinking restless young ladies cause problems too?

"I want to keep the children occupied."

"How so?"

"While the Lakota women are with Esmeralda Monroe, I would like to entertain them."

"Very commendable. Perhaps a puppet show? But why do you ask me?" His eyes were darting over the sea of paper. He couldn't wait to get started again.

She hadn't expected it to be so easy. But it was only easy because he was very busy with what he considered bigger problems and she had skirted the truth. She could stand up now, excuse herself, and begin teaching the Lakota children almost immediately. All she had to do was walk out the door, gather some children together, and start teaching them the English alphabet. The Indian Agent wouldn't find out about it for a long time.

Holly took another deep breath. "What I meant was I would

like to teach them."

"Teach them!" He rose from his chair. "Whew! I didn't know that's what you meant." He walked to the window and stared outside as if he expected to see a little red schoolhouse that sprang up overnight.

"Yes, Mr. Irwin. I would like to teach them the rudiments of English, as well as geography, and so forth."

"Like regular children?" He frowned.

"Yes, sir. Attendance would be strictly voluntary. And I would not indoctrinate them in religion. A minister could instruct them in that if you desire that. I would remain as low-key as possible. The children would cause less trouble for you in the future, Mr. Irwin. In fact I think the Indian Bureau would be very impressed with you for initiating such an enlightened project."

He turned and smiled. "And here I thought you were just a pretty face. You are quite as clever as any man, Miss Bennington."

Thanks to Esmeralda, thought Holly. "I wish only to teach the children." The truth was so easy to say. It bubbled out like pure spring water.

"It's going to be very difficult to get very far with the children. The Lakotas are nomads. They come and go like the wind."

"Then they need new options."

"You seem to be a young lady that cherishes the truth, Miss Bennington."

"I certainly pray for that every day, sir." What was he getting at?

"What if I choose not to approve your project but benignly neglect it? What would you say to an inquisitive Army officer who asked you what you were doing with these Lakota children?"

So that was it. Another deception. It would be so easy to agree. Agent Irwin was saying, Yes, but if you get caught don't tell anyone I said yes.

Holly thought hard for a biblical answer. Jesus wanted His

disciples to be as wise as serpents. Did that mean they could be slightly dishonest if they helped a greater good? She doubted it, but she wasn't sure. Had Jesus ever been dishonest? She couldn't think of one instance of Him being dishonest. So to live in Christ, one could not be slightly dishonest. Perhaps though one could be silent. Hadn't Jesus been silent when questioned? Hadn't He once or twice answered a question with another question? Perhaps she could just remain silent. Yes, the more she thought about it the more sure of it she became. She was shocked as she realized that this was the first time she had truly made a decision while trying to live in Christ.

"If questioned I will refuse to answer," Holly announced to the Indian Agent.

"Oh no!" His eyes were huge. "No, Miss Bennington, you must not only take full blame but clear me as well."

"Then I will say you did not approve it. That's true, isn't it?"

"I don't know." He looked at all the papers waiting on his desk. "Oh, for heaven's sakes, go ahead." He waved her out of his office. "But don't drag me into it when the army finds out."

The parable of the persistent widow popped into Holly's mind as she headed toward the Lakota women's garden that was plotted out just beyond the trader's building and the agent's office. Esmeralda was as happy about Holly's success as she was. Esmeralda agreed to be mute about it if questioned. That reassured Holly that she was doing the right thing. After all, Esmeralda was the daughter of the post commander!

Holly began teaching the children the alphabet that morning. How quickly they caught on. And of course her precious little Red Wing was in the front row working on her ABC's like a tyro.

All Holly's doubts and fears about Jonah Finch evaporated. She had been so foolish to wallow in her own problems. Still, she looked for Jonah during the day. It was hard to imagine either Granville or Jonah not stopping in at the trader's building sometime during the day. And the main road into the village went right past the garden. Then she realized she hadn't seen Granville since Saturday. While that was unusual, his absence didn't carry the dull aching thud in the chest that Jonah's absence carried.

That evening Holly half-expected a knock on the door while she labored over the next day's lesson for the children. Surely Jonah would call on her. Then she would be quite hostile to him. Of course that was the only reason she anticipated it so eagerly, she told herself. After all, she certainly couldn't blister him with her disapproval if he didn't even show up.

But he didn't show up. And the next morning she was back in the village teaching the children while Esmeralda worked with the Lakota women in the garden. The first day Holly had eleven children who participated. This time there were fourteen children.

A brave appeared, with his blanket over his face. He stood there, as rigid and silent as a stone.

Holly was glad she had planned the game she did. It was a two-way road. Holly would pick up something like a stick and say the English word for it. Then the children would say the Lakota word for it and also make the sign for it. Holly had brought a basket full of many small items from the cottage. She hoped Hop Fong wouldn't miss some of them from the kitchen. The children went through all of them, too. Finally the brave left, and Holly knew if he approved of what she was doing he would not return the next day. If he didn't approve, he would return, probably with several other braves, to watch her.

That evening she again waited for the knock on the door. She tried to convince herself it was only because Franklin was gone. But in her darkest moments, she ached for Jonah. Why was he avoiding her? She had not condemned him. Yes, she had said she wanted to separate for a while. But didn't he know she was only half-serious? Where was he? She relived the kiss in the buggy a thousand times. Yes, she really had almost swooned. It was overwhelmingly pleasant.

And the longer she waited, the more she loved Jonah.

She had caused the separation. Just because they met some

Lakotas out for a ride. What had Jonah said? They were merely looking out for horse thieves. Mrs. Monroe had told her there were horse thieves. Agent Irwin had said the same thing. Why had she been so rough on Jonah? Why didn't he come to see her?

The next day, Holly submerged her longing for Jonah by teaching the children. She thanked God that no braves came to watch her. She and the children worked with numbers. Holly felt she should vary the lessons as much as possible. She found that the Lakota used a system of tens. And the children understood numbers up to a thousand readily. They even had a sign for one thousand.

Next they explained their ages. They did not give their age in years but in winters. Red Wing said she was five winters old. Billy Boudreau said sarcastically that young Lakotas didn't care how old they were and old Lakotas didn't want to know how old they were. But Holly noticed how engrossed Billy was becoming in the lessons they did. He was truly starved for the white man's learning. If anyone needed to know the white man's ways, it was Billy, stuck between two worlds.

Noticing that Red Wing was not her usual bubbly self, Holly took her aside while the other children were having lunch.

"Are you sad?" asked Holly, at the same time signing it.

Red Wing repeated the sign of taking her heart and throwing it on the ground. "Very sad."

"Why?"

Red Wing held her elbows out in front of her with her forearms straight up. She held her palms toward each other. Then she seesawed her palms back and forth past each other.

"A fight?" asked Holly.

Red Wing nodded. She held her palms together and then spread her arms far apart.

Holly gasped, "A big fight?" She signed for Red Wing's parents and made it a question by shrugging.

Red Wing shook her head, no. She motioned across the entire village. Then she turned and motioned toward the army camp.

Holly didn't want to believe her. "A war? Between the Lakotas and the army? Why would there be a war?" Holly signed.

Red Wing went through the motion of loading shells into a rifle. Then she put the imaginary rifle to her shoulder and pumped an imaginary lever several times. She made the signs for *new* and *many*.

Holly gasped. "Many new repeating rifles?"

Red Wing said, "Yes! Many." And she signed repeating rifle again. This time she added popping sounds.

"How do you know?" Holly held her hand palm down by her left breast, then flung her hand to the right and flipped it over.

Red Wing looked at the ground and hung her head.

"Your father?"

Red Wing huffed and stomped her foot so hard the dust flew. Her small hands were fists.

"Your mother?"

Red Wing huffed and stomped her foot again.

Holly asked Red Wing about the trader Louis Boudreau, then his wife Running Lark, then cousin Billy Boudreau, then Red Wing's brother, and then her grandparents. Each time Red Wing huffed and stomped dust off the ground. Holly was about to sneeze. Red Wing would not volunteer the source of her information to Holly. That meant the source was someone Red Wing liked. But Holly had named everyone.

Well, not everyone. She had seen Red Wing with Jonah once. But of course it couldn't be Jonah.

Dread crawled on Holly like a hairy spider. She said fearfully, "Was it Jonah?"

Red Wing kept her eyes on the ground.

Holly repeated herself, "Was it Jonah?" This time she made the sign for a man, then rubbed her face for the color red and pointed at her own hair. Was it a redheaded man?

Red Wing ran back to the other children.

Holly's heart ached as if it would break.

fourteen

Jonah, truly a gunrunner?

Holly was numb the rest of the afternoon. Her mind stumbled along, making excuse after excuse for Jonah. After all, Red Wing could have just heard a rumor about Jonah gunrunning, or she could have heard Jonah talking to someone else about gunrunning. Or perhaps Jonah questioned Red Wing about gunrunners and the girl misunderstood him.

Holly thought about the situation through Hop Fong's pepper beef and the rest of the evening, too. She was glad Franklin was not there. Could she have kept such a secret to herself?

The facts began to add up. First of all, Blabby had said Jonah wasn't straight. Jonah himself said Blabby didn't lie. Secondly, Jonah seemed to have no visible means of supporting himself. A criminal like a gunrunner certainly would not want his means visible. Thirdly, the nasty Lakota brave Muddy Haunch—or was he Bloody Hawk?—knew Jonah had a new repeating rifle. Yet Jonah had the rifle out of sight under the seat of the buggy.

She tried to defeat her own arguments. But as she cycled back through the logic, she just added more arguments against Jonah. The man at Camp Clarke joked about Jonah's freight wagon always being so heavy it must be full of cannon balls. It may have always been that heavy because it was loaded with rifles and ammunition. Holly had hefted a rifle or two. They were very heavy. And anyone would know the ammunition was even heavier. Oh, and they were run down by the three dark filthy men on the trail! She had actually forgotten them. They had expected to meet Jonah somewhere that day, but he had been delayed. Why? Because the shipment of rifles from the East was a day late!

131

There was a knock on the door.

Before she could get there, the door opened and in walked Franklin. "Hello. Hello. Home at last." He was smiling.

"Hello," she said numbly. She tried to smile but she was profoundly depressed.

"You're not in very good spirits. Are you still sick from Sunday?"

"No." Should she tell him about Jonah?

"What's wrong then? Tell me about it."

This was her chance. Oh, what a relief it would be to dump her doubts and fears on someone else. Why not her big brother? But she hesitated. Somehow she knew this problem was her trial alone—at least for a while. It would measure how big a person she had become. Somehow she had to cope with it alone a little longer.

She smiled pleasantly, as she knew Esmeralda would, to hide the pain. "It's fatigue, pure and simple. We've been working very hard in the village." And she added perkily, "We have so many projects going!"

"Have you had supper?"

"Yes. I wasn't sure you'd be back. Esmeralda told me a three-day scout can end up being twice as long as that."

"You had best go to bed, little sister. I've never seen you look so tired."

"Good advice, big brother. Good night." She was glad to go into her bedroom. She couldn't hide her depression any longer, and she didn't want to lie about it. She needed more time to think. She read the Scriptures. She searched for a passage she remembered on resolving disputes. She was sure it was in one of Paul's letters.

Finally she stopped looking. She remembered the essence of it. There was only one thing for her to do: confront Jonah. Either he could explain all the incriminating facts or he could not explain them. And then Holly would act accordingly. If Jonah were innocent, her joy would be unbounded. If Jonah were guilty, she could grieve her betrayed love. But she also owed it to the camp and the Lakotas to prevent the bloodshed that would certainly happen if renegade Lakotas got the smuggled rifles.

The next morning she managed to be cheerful for Franklin at breakfast. It was almost easy now that she had made a decision. After Franklin left, Billy Boudreau and Esmeralda arrived in the buggy for Holly. And on the way to the village, Esmeralda's sunny optimism bolstered Holly. And not once did she ask what was troubling Holly. It was as if Esmeralda knew this trouble if mentioned too soon would consume everyone.

In the village Holly entertained the children with alphabet games. They took turns scratching the letters of the alphabet into the scrabbly dirt beside the garden. They would say the letter aloud. And Holly would name some object that began with the letter and they would all say the name aloud.

But when the sun was still so low that even Red Wing cast a giant shadow, Holly heard horses clop up to the trader's building. They carried Granville and Jonah. Jonah looked as normal as ever. Granville wore his bizarre costume again. The two men dismounted and tied the horses to a hitching rail. Holly waited for Granville to rush inside the trader's building. It was strange how predictable he was.

Her heart was hammering as she walked over to Jonah. He cupped his hand to feed oats to his big bay. Then he did the same for the other horse.

"Jonah!" she called.

"Holly?" He acted as if everything was normal.

"I need to talk to you."

"I hope you're pleased," he said. "I stayed away, just as you requested."

"Come with me." She walked under a lean-to where the trader had his mule tied. Jonah followed her. She swirled to face him. "I want the truth," she pleaded.

"About what?"

"About who you are. About what you do here."

"I'm Jonah Finch. I do odd jobs."

"I don't believe you." She waited for him to speak but he didn't. She felt her anger grow. "I trusted my heart to you. You betrayed me."

"But how?"

"I heard from a completely reliable source that you are smuggling new repeating rifles to the Lakotas…to that nasty Lakota warrior Muddy Haunch. No! His name is Bloody Hawk—like I thought he was called all along."

Jonah glanced around. "Who have you told about this?"

"No one yet."

"Do you love me?"

"How can you ask such a question?"

"I love you, Holly."

"What?" She became speechless. All her life she'd dreamed about the ecstasy of hearing those three words. Words of endearing love for her alone. And now they came to her from a villain!

"I really thought you loved me," he said.

"I do!" she blurted. There. The truth was out. But what an awful truth it was. She was a tragic figure to be sure. Even now she wanted to throw herself into his arms. She wanted to smother her pain with kisses.

He held her by the shoulders. "The story you heard is not true. You must trust me. A day or two is all. I'll explain everything then. Don't tell anyone. If you really love me you'll not tell anyone."

She heard the crunch of boots on gravel. It was Granville. Had he been listening? "Holly!" he exclaimed. "I haven't seen you in a raccoon's age as they quaintly say out here. Or is it a possum's age?"

"May I borrow your horse, Granville?"

"Yes, but—"

"Thank you," she cried and hiked up her skirts to dash to Granville's small black horse. She grabbed the reins and mounted it awkwardly in her long skirt. She guessed Jonah had picked it out for Granville because it was exceptionally gentle and responsive. And she was right. The horse was a small marvel. The slightest touch of Holly's knee and the horse surged ahead. The gentlest vibration on the reins and it turned. She could ride well. Even if Papa had overprotected her, somehow she'd still learned to ride well. It must have been his blind spot.

She forgot how much she liked to ride. She headed toward the bluffs. The horse was lively. Even in her cloud of anger and confusion she knew she had never ridden a horse with such speed before. She wanted the horse to blister across the plains. But she kept it to a trot. Somehow she worried about the animal. More than herself.

She rode along the border between the village and the camp. The countryside was dangerous and Esmeralda had warned her this no-man's land was the most dangerous of all. She was too angry to worry about danger. Once she looked back. Far behind her a rider was following her. That was why she didn't ride up into the bluffs. She wasn't that foolish. She stopped and got off the horse. She looked back. The rider had stopped too. Did he ride a bay? She couldn't tell.

She dropped the reins. She knew this horse was a wonderful horse. Yes, Jonah had picked it. The horse would not leave her. And the calm animal immediately began to graze. The animal softened her anger. She patted its warm side and sat down in the short buffalo grass. She carefully arranged her dress under herself. She was not so angry any more that she wanted the stickery grass to stab her. She sat Indian-style facing the bluffs.

Dark pines covered the crest of the bluffs. She desperately wanted to be up there where she could almost touch the clouds. She had to be alone with God. And it would seem heavenly up there she was sure. But she soon admitted to herself that was childish. She could find God anywhere. He was never away from His children. She bowed her head.

"What am I to do, heavenly Father? Send me a sign. Jonah asked me to trust him. Yet I know he's involved in something very evil. Innocent people could be killed. But if I tell on Jonah, he might go to prison. What if he were innocent but my testimony sent him to prison anyway? What am I to do?"

She was calmer now. Focusing on thoughts of Jesus and His love for her, she waited for the answer to her prayer. When other thoughts intruded, she quickly scatted them away and focused on Jesus. Time was frozen.

Suddenly she was aware she was staring at the bluffs. Time had begun again. She jumped up. It startled her horse. What a feeling she had! It was unrelenting joy.

She remembered the events of the day. But she felt detached from them. The sun was higher. How long had she been praying? An hour? Two hours? She saw movement high in the bluffs. A rider. No, several riders. One after another they appeared and disappeared among the pine trees—like fish in a moss-tufted pool. They were headed west. They seemed to be descending, too. Somehow she knew they were Lakotas. It was ironic, but she had to thank the lone rider for making her afraid to ride up into the bluffs.

She turned to look south. The lone rider in the distance was still there. She calmly mounted the black horse and with a slight nudge of her knee and a tiny movement of the rein, she started it into a slow trot toward camp. The route took her away from the rider. The rider must have been watching her. Holly didn't know what she was going to do, but she was confident that once she reached the camp God would let her know.

She dismounted in front of the cottage and tied the black horse to a hitching post. Someone was on the porch.

"Holly!" It was Granville.

"Yes?" she answered uncertainly. Granville was so far out of her thoughts, she had to stop to think why he might be there. He jumped off the porch and took off his ten-gallon hat with a flourish.

"Holly, I have a wonderful idea." Granville never stayed silent long. "Now don't say no until you've heard me out. Come and sit by me on the porch." He took her hand and led her to a chair on the porch. "Sit right here, my dear." He plopped down next to her and leaned over. "Don't think I've forgotten why you wanted me to come here, dearest. I want to emphasize that cogent fact before I tell you I've decided I can't abide this desolation here any longer. I'm a thoroughbred here tripping over donkeys. But I don't want to race off without you."

"What do you mean?" Holly had forgotten all about her earlier scheming. It seemed ages ago.

"I want to marry you."

"Marry!" Its absurdity exploded from her.

"Yes. Marry me. You don't think I would ask you to leave here with me without doing the honorable thing, do you?"

"Do you mean you want to marry me right here at the camp?"

"Oh no, dearest. We would have to marry in Philadelphia. I couldn't leave my dear mother out of the most important day of my life. Surely you understand that?"

"Yes." Holly's head was swimming. She was actually considering his proposal. She could learn to love Granville, she supposed. After all, she trusted her feelings with Jonah and got her heart broken into a million pieces. Perhaps Granville was her destiny. Hadn't he appeared at the exact moment— perhaps the only moment in her life—she would consider such a proposal? Why shouldn't she commit to marriage the safe way? Why shouldn't she accept a proposal from a man who was pleasant and well off, even if she didn't love him yet. A dull safe relationship couldn't be any worse than the sordid relationship she had with Jonah.

"What do you say, dearest?" Granville's face was screwed up around his monocle trying to decipher her face.

Reveal the truth, she told herself. *Include this man. Let him share her ordeal. Test him.*

She looked at him expectantly. "I have to do something here first."

"What could be so important as to come before our love and our sweet happiness?"

"I think Jonah Finch is involved in gunrunning."

"No!" Granville's monocle popped out of his eye and dangled off his cheek.

"Yes. I have to tell Franklin."

"Tell Franklin!"

"Of course. I've thought about it a great deal."

"Th...th...think about your action again, my dear," he sputtered. "You will become a key witness. There will be a trial. You will be tied up here in the wilderness for weeks. No, for months!"

"But I must."

"I can't wait another day, another hour, dearest. I'm absolutely distraught with this wilderness. You must come with me today."

"Today?"

"It can be arranged immediately." Granville seemed distant now. It was as if he were negotiating the purchase of a horse and trying to appear indifferent. "Franklin will understand. You're nineteen, dearest, not exactly the freshest bloom on the tree."

"I must think!" Holly jumped up angrily and ran inside. She slammed the door. The dolt! Granville's insensitivity jolted her out of her insane rationale for marrying him.

Through the closed door she heard Granville. "Holly! Why are you so upset? Calm down, dearest. I'll be back. Just promise me you won't do anything for a while. Give me until this evening. Better yet, give me until tomorrow morning. Please! Don't tell Franklin or I won't be able to take you away from this wilderness nightmare, dearest."

Silence hung heavy as she listened through the door. She never heard his heavy boots clomping off the porch. So he was at the door listening, too.

"I'll think about it!" she yelled. The heavy boots clomped off the porch. At last the silence was safe and real, not the silence of some lurking thing. She wrapped herself in it.

What was she going to do? Granville was probably a little bit right. She could be tied up for a few days. And he threatened to leave camp right away. He was her only chance to get out of the wilderness, and she wanted to leave the wilderness. No. It was Jonah she wanted to leave. She didn't want to leave Red Wing and the children.

The shrill notes of a bugle reached her. Time for lunch in the camp. The hall clock bonged twelve times. It was noon. The day wasn't even half over. It was the longest day of her life. Hadn't she been up for a hundred hours?

What was she going to do?

Reveal the truth, something told her. And she already knew to whom she had to reveal the truth.

She felt her body relax.

Yes, the ordeal would soon be over. Franklin would be coming home for lunch any second.

fifteen

The front door opened. Franklin stopped in his tracks and gaped at Holly. "What are you doing here? Why aren't you in the village? Why is the black Arabian tied up outside? What's going on?"

"Oh, Franklin!" Holly ran and threw her arms around his neck. "It's so awful."

"Did something bad happen in the village? Is Esmeralda all right? Tell me. Quick. Is she all right?"

"Esmeralda is fine," she bawled. "It's Jonah. He's a gunrunner!"

Franklin plopped down on the sofa as if he were very tired and ran his fingers through his hair. Holly thought she heard him groan.

"Why do you think that?" he asked wearily.

She stood over him. "A Lakota girl told me she overheard Jonah talking about new repeating rifles."

"How old is she?" he asked wearily.

"Four. No. Five."

"All of five years old?" Franklin smothered a smile.

"There's much more to incriminate Jonah than that," Holly snapped defensively. "He drives a freight wagon full of rifles and ammunition. He practically collapsed the bridge at Camp Clarke."

"Oh, Holly dear, that yahoo in the derby hat at Camp Clarke is always trying to charge everybody extra by saying the wagon is too heavy and it's going to bust his boss's bridge."

Holly blinked in frustration. Those were almost the exact words of the man in the derby. "I remember something else. At that station between Camp Clarke and here the stock tender

140

Blabby Campbell said there was something crooked about Jonah."

"Are you sure he didn't just say there was something about Jonah he couldn't figure out?"

"What?" She was stumped. "I can't remember his exact words. But wait a minute. We met three very dark filthy men on the trail. They were old friends of Jonah's."

"I told you before that appearances out here can fool a refined person from the East."

"All right! But listen to this. Sunday when we were out in the buggy—"

"Who was in the buggy?"

"Jonah and I."

Franklin smiled. "So you two were out a courtin'? Is Jonah sparking you?" The smile spread into a wide, teasing grin.

"This is serious, mister. We were stopped by ten very nasty looking Lakota warriors. One was called Bloody Hawk. He asked to see Jonah's repeating rifle. A Winchester Model 73, I think you called it. And when it was all over, Jonah acted like it was nothing. And he even tried to convince me the warrior's name was Muddy Haunch!"

"Yes, I know a Muddy Haunch. He does look nasty. But he's a harmless fellow—all bark and no bite. He and his friends were probably out watching for horse thieves."

"Or perhaps picking flowers!" Holly became exasperated "You aren't convinced at all, are you? What is going on around here?"

"I just want to be sure of the facts. There are so many rumors on an Army post."

"If you don't report it to the post commander, I most certainly will!"

"I'm sorry, Holly. Of course it must be reported. I'm very glad you told me. I'll report it at once to the post commander." He stood up. "Right after lunch."

"Should you wait? You might miss him."

"He's at his house for lunch. I saw him go inside."

Holly sat in the kitchen and watched Franklin eat steak and eggs. She guessed this was the way soldiers reacted to colossally difficult news. They learned even in battle a man still has to eat. A man still has to sleep even if he's expecting a fierce battle the next day. After all, Franklin had fought in the battle of Rosebud against the mighty Crazy Horse. How could she not trust a veteran soldier like Franklin?

"What should I do?" she asked.

"Thank you for asking." He wiped his mouth with his napkin. "Nothing. Do not contact Jonah. Or anyone else."

She remembered Granville. "Granville has been around here today. He's coming back."

"Granville?" Franklin didn't seem very surprised. "Why was he here?"

"Let me think…" Should she tell the truth? It was so personal. And besides, she was still a little miffed at how Franklin had received her electrifying news about Jonah. Why should she let Franklin deflate her any more today? He wouldn't think Granville's proposal was important. Unless she acted like she was going to accept. The more she thought about it the more she realized how disconcerting it would be to Franklin if she did want to leave with Granville. That would shake him up. It was tempting.

"I have to leave right away. Can't you remember?"

"It slipped my mind."

"Well, try to remember."

"I will." Why was it suddenly so important to Franklin? He looked positively bulldogish. She didn't want to tell him the truth. But how tired she was of lying. How had her life changed so that she couldn't get through one day without lying?. "I wish I could remember," she lied. "I guess it wasn't very important."

"You had better not talk to him any more today." Franklin was not even civil now. He was pink in anger.

"Why?"

"Well, dear sister, you might say something about Jonah

Finch like you said to me. And it's really best if you give me a chance to take care of this." He was clenching his teeth.

"And the post commander, too?"

"Yes. It's best if you give me and the post commander a chance to confront Jonah and get this dubious business straightened out."

He opened the front door. "I better take his horse."

"Don't!"

"Why?" He turned, amazed.

"Because if he comes back for it and it's gone, he will be sure to come to the door to ask about it."

Franklin frowned skeptically. "All right. I'll leave it." And he walked toward a horse tied to another hitching post. The horse was white, mottled brown. It looked like some of the Lakota horses, but it was much larger.

"What kind of horse is that, Franklin?"

"Appaloosa."

She closed the door and sat down. She didn't puzzle over Franklin's odd horse. She had too many other things on her mind. The thought of the black horse still being there was soothing to her for some reason. The hall clock said ten minutes before one. It had been a long day. Somehow she sensed a lifetime remained in the rest of the day. Why?

She had to think. Franklin might be an experienced soldier but she knew what she had seen and heard far better than he did. Did she believe Jonah was guilty or not?

And if she did, what would she do about it?

Once again Holly worked her way through the pros and cons of Jonah Finch. As she did, her heart sank. He was definitely involved in gunrunning. So she had to do something. She decided that she would wait until two o'clock, then if she had not changed her mind, she herself would visit the post commander!

She would be clever about it. She wouldn't rush in hysterical. No, she was only wanted confirmation that action was being taken. She both dreaded and looked forward to what she had to do. One month ago, she wouldn't have attempted it.

Holly looked outside. The black horse tugged at her conscience. Jonah would never neglect an animal that long. She went outside and led the horse around back. She had the strangest feeling she was doing it for some reason other than simple kindness.

Hop Fong was working in his garden. "Missy, want oats for horse? I get forage bag." His smile was forced as he warily watched her lead the horse clopping oh-so-close to his vegetables.

Holly found a pan and gave the horse water. Then Hop Fong put a forage bag over its head and dumped in some oats. The gentle head munched oats as Holly tied the lead from its halter to the cottage on the east side so the horse would be shaded and couldn't stray into Hop Fong's vegetables. The big eyes of the horse seemed even bigger with gratitude.

How she liked that gentle, intelligent horse. How she dreaded it when the clock bonged twice while she sat on the sofa inside. "So it really has come to this!" she cried out. She freshened up, grabbed a parasol, and walked outside. She strolled down the walk toward the house of the post commander.

"Why, Miss Bennington!" It was Mrs. Monroe who opened the door. "Come in. How nice of you to visit. But I thought you were with Esmeralda. Everything is all right, isn't it? Esmeralda is all right, isn't she?"

"Oh, of course. I left because I was overcome with heat." Anger was heat—in a way. But Holly knew it was another lie.

"Yes, it's so scorchingly hot out. How did Franklin like his scout? What did he think about going right back out on another one? I saw a lovely little black horse in front of your cottage. Is it yours?"

Holly blinked as if the darkness of the house blinded her, but it was really a reaction to the tumult of questions. She didn't know which question to answer first, and she had to know for sure if Franklin had been there.

She asked rather pointedly, "Is the commander in? I don't wish to disturb his lunch."

"Oh, my dear, he's never here at two o'clock."

"Oh." Holly felt relief. Colonel Monroe had probably rushed out. She was almost sure of it. But still, she should be certain. Why was she so stubborn? "Did he rush out with Franklin?" She noticed Mrs. Monroe's shocked reaction. "I just meant I thought I saw the two of them together."

Mrs. Monroe held her arms up. "But my dear, the colonel hasn't even been in the camp since yesterday."

"What?" Holly saw disapproval cloud Mrs. Monroe's face and realized she was being impertinent. She must tone down her questions. She must be shrewd and not crude. "I'm so sorry," she added cheerily. "I really thought I saw the two of them. And I reacted so brusquely because I was wondering if perhaps I might have been in the sun too long this morning." She dabbed her forehead with her hanky and made her face look drained. Lying was becoming all too easy.

"Oh, you poor young dear. Sit down. Of course it's the heat. You're out there with the mad dogs and Englishmen."

Holly laughed. "Yes, you're right. I'm trying to do too much." What else had Mrs. Monroe said? Was Franklin going on another scout? She said cautiously, "Why, I'd even forgotten Franklin was leaving on another scout."

"Oh, you poor, poor dear. Yes, I saw him racing out of here with his entire A-troop not more than half an hour ago.

"Are you sure it was Franklin?"

"Yes, my dear," said Mrs. Monroe with some exasperation but with good humor. "Your brother rides the only Appaloosa in the camp."

"Which way did they go?"

"I don't know." Her good humor was fast disappearing.

"What about a red-haired man? Did you see him riding out of the camp too?" Holly realized she had really stepped over the boundary of good manners. She was almost saying Mrs. Monroe was a snoop who peaked out her window to watch what everyone was doing.

Mrs. Monroe put her hands on her ample hips. Her face was

pinched. "Yes, as matter of fact I saw a red-haired man ride south. There. Are you satisfied? Now I suggest you go to your cottage and take a nice long nap!"

Mrs. Monroe took her by the elbow and before Holly could mend one of the many fences that she had torn down, she was standing outside watching the door close in her face.

"I'd better be right," she muttered and walked back toward the cottage. "Franklin may be a private before the day is over."

Once again she sat in the living room. *Give me strength, Lord,* she prayed. Franklin had lied to her. He never saw the colonel go inside his house for lunch. Franklin certainly never told the colonel her concerns about Jonah. Jonah rode south. What did it all mean?

She remembered the Lakota in the bluffs. They were going west. No, they were descending as they went west. They could be staying out of sight as they skirted the camp to the west before they headed south. That would certainly be the direction toward a cache of rifles hidden by gunrunners smuggling rifles from Sidney. That was quite a string of assumptions. Could she be right? If she was right, something very big and very bad was happening. Today.

What could she do about it?

Tell Franklin? She had tried that and failed.

Tell the post commander? He wasn't available.

Tell the Indian Agent at the village? She would only get him killed.

Tell Esmeralda? She wouldn't believe her, and what if she did?

Tell Granville? She already had.

There was no one left to tell. There was no one who could help her.

No! There was someone!

Holly raced into Franklin's office and began clawing through the cardboard boxes. Where were they? She hadn't worn them in over a year. She had almost forgotten them. But she needed them now. Yes, there they were!

She clutched them to her breast and ran to her bedroom. She shed her dress and tugged on the riding pants. She could barely get them on. Had she gotten so fat in one year? She looked at herself in the mirror. No, she wasn't fat. Not even plump. Not even baby-fattish. She was a woman with the hips of a woman.

She pulled on the blouse that went with the riding pants. It was very tight. She didn't have to look in the mirror. She wanted to. She would have delighted in it. The girl/almost woman had become a woman.

She pulled on the boots. They fit just as perfectly as they always did. Just further proof. The stem hadn't changed but the rose had bloomed. She had to make time to look at herself in the mirror. Oh, how she had bloomed! She looked rounded like she remembered Mama looking.

Holly felt tragic, too. This could be a very bad day for a young tender blossom. Surely the bloom would last.

She pulled a vest over her blouse, donned a smart riding cap, and slipped out the front door so she wouldn't disturb Hop Fong. She crept around the east side of the house and quietly untied the black horse.

Holly mounted and rode out the front. She veered left into a soft walk toward the village. As she left the last of the camp facilities behind, she nudged the horse into a trot, then a canter, then an all out gallop.

Heads were all directed at her as she reined the horse to stop at the garden beyond the trader's building. She swung down from the horse.

"Holly!" Esmeralda was gaping. "You've put on a riding habit. And you rode up here like you're on Paul Revere's ride! Is something wrong?"

"Yes, but I can't explain. Where is Red Wing?"

Red Wing came running. Her face was bright with excitement. Holly knew what she was thinking. Holly had been with the Lakotas too much not to know Red Wing thought Holly was even more wonderful than she thought she was before. Why, Holly rode a horse like a warrior. It was even a small nimble horse like the Lakota rode. Red Wing's eyes bugged at Holly's pants. Holly wore breeches like a man! What a day for Red Wing! How much more could she take in one day? Red Wing began laughing with glee.

Holly mounted again and reached down to sweep Red Wing up onto the horse. Holly called to Esmeralda, "Don't worry. I'll bring her right back."

She urged the horse into the village.

Heads followed her. Holly wanted to ride like the wind. Her plan could still fall apart a hundred different ways. But she had to slow the horse to a walk. The Lakota, so private and unperturbable, were shocked to see this rider carrying Red Wing through the village. Every brave gawked at her as he realized she was a woman. And no brave could mistake Holly for a man for more than a second.

She saw the big tepee with the yellow stripes. *Lord help me and Red Wing,* she prayed. *Please let me remember my signs.*

She quietly dismounted a short distance from the tepee. She took Red Wing's hand and walked around to the east side of the tepee.

Red Wing pointed to the flap. It was open. Holly knew that meant anyone inside would receive visitors. But one had to speak first. One had to ask permission to enter.

Holly called shakily, "We wish to enter."

Of course anyone inside would not understand her. But she wanted to make sure whoever was inside knew she was coming. It was not a soldier coming through the flap. It was a woman.

Red Wing said something to the open flap, too.

Good, sighed Holly, *whoever was at home would know a Lakota child was there, too. And what harm could a child do?*

She took a deep breath, prayed for protection, squeezed Red Wing's hand, and bent over. She crawled through the open flap. Red Wing scuffled in right beside her.

sixteen

Red Wing gasped, *"Tashunka witko!"*

"Yes," murmured Holly. "He is Crazy Horse."

He sat at the far west side of the tepee, smoking a long red pipe. He was a silhouette, backlit by the glow of the afternoon sun through the hide of the tepee. Raw sunlight streamed in the smoke hole above and lit up Holly and Red Wing.

Holly felt icy calm. The silence in the tepee was deep. It seemed permanent. She remembered her first visit. She was terrified then. She thought she was going to see a demon as dazzling as Lucifer and instead she saw a great warrior.

She and Red Wing walked in tiny steps to the left of the dead fire in the center of the tepee. Now Holly saw that Crazy Horse wore a red breechcloth over blue denim pants. Red garters held the upper sleeves of his white shirt puffed out. He wore brown moccasins. A white choker circled his neck. His face was young and very light-skinned. His hair was a soft tan color, parted in the middle and hanging to his waist in long, thick braids. Two reddish brown feathers were in his hair, one straight up and one hanging off to the side.

Holly squeezed Red Wing's hand and walked closer. Now Holly saw his face was sharp and scarred. Once she had thought he looked boyish. But she saw now he carried many battles on his skin. His hands were gentle with the pipe, but the scars and crooked fingers betrayed savage strength. His eyes were a million miles away. He was a free man anywhere. No one could capture a man like Crazy Horse. And yet he must have ached for his people who could not be free like he was.

Holly began to tremble. But it wasn't from fear.

She nudged Red Wing forward. "Tell him what you told me."

And Holly made the sign for repeating rifles.

For the tiniest moment Holly thought she saw him glance at the small girl. But she wasn't sure. He seemed absolutely impenetrable.

Red Wing sat down, primly folding her legs to the side and arranging her buckskin dress over her legs. She turned to give Holly an exasperated look. Holly sat down too, careful to sit exactly the same way. It was some kind of etiquette for women that had to be observed.

Only then did Red Wing begin to talk and make signs. She was scared, and her signs were small and crabbed. But after a few moments she began to loosen up. Holly breathed a sigh of relief. Red Wing was telling the story about the rifles. She even rubbed her face once as she held out a braid to make the sign for red hair. But Crazy Horse said nothing. He didn't even blink. Finally Red Wing stopped talking.

Holly patted Red Wing's arm. Now it was her turn. Her throat was dry as sand. She must not sound hysterical. She must sound confident and certain.

She said, "I see many Lakotas head south today." And she labored through all the signs as she repeated the sentence over and over. Surely he understood her.

But he never even blinked.

"They go south for rifles." And Holly made the sign for a repeating rifle, although she wasn't sure she was doing it right. So she made the sign again. Her voice grew bolder with sincerity.

There was no response. Holly had to take a chance. She closed her fist except for her index and middle finger. She held her fist over her chin with the two fingers under her nostrils. Her hand moved away and down to the right: the sign for *blood.* Then she took a deep breath and moved over slowly and touched the hawk feather that stood straight up from his hair. Did he understand her?

"You look!" she cried as she signed it too. Then she repeated what she thought was "Bloody Hawk," reaching over and touching his hawk feather. Did he grunt? Or was it a groan from Red Wing? Holly repeated the sign again and then made the sign for repeating rifles. Did he understand her? She would keep repeating it over and over. She would go back to her first sentence. She would do it until—

Crazy Horse tapped his pipe on the floor of the tepee!

"We go!" yipped Red Wing.

"Yes," gulped Holly. "I know. When the host empties his pipe that is the sign for the guests to leave." Holly almost tripped over Red Wing backing up.

Outside, the air hit her like a bucket of cold water. She grabbed Red Wing and quickly walked to the black horse. She was perspiring. It was the cold sweat of fear. She had actually stood in front of one of the great warriors of the ages. She, Holly Bennington. She had spoken to Crazy Horse. But she felt dead inside. Did he not understand what she was saying? Or did he understand and not care? It was obvious he wasn't going to do anything. So she had failed.

What was she to do now?

There was no point in lingering in the village. It would only cause suspicions. There was no one else she wanted to tell her story to. Running around the village telling any Lakota who would listen about certain Lakota warriors and rifles would undermine all Esmeralda's good works. Holly mounted and took Red Wing back to the garden. She gently lowered her to the ground.

Esmeralda called, "What in the world are you doing?"

"I must go," answered Holly, and she nudged the horse into a trot toward the camp.

God, what should I do now? Holly prayed. She had done everything. Everything had failed. *Oh please, God, don't let the Lakota warriors get new repeating rifles. Please don't let there be a battle. Please don't let Jonah be involved.*

Suddenly she reined in the horse. Praying was an absolute

necessity, all right, but she was also sure that God needed His children to act as well as pray. Paul, Mary, David, Rahab, Peter, and all the others she admired so much in Scripture were people of action. They took the risks that were necessary to do God's will.

Camp Robinson lay to the west. Holly nudged the horse south. She didn't want to ride through the camp. Someone might detain her. Probably by now rumors were flying and everyone was convinced she had gone crazy. Even Granville might stop her. After all, she had his horse.

She couldn't allow herself to be stopped. She wasn't whipped yet.

She let the horse drink from a creek, then rode furiously south. The trail that ran between the camp and Sidney could not be that far off. The gunrunners must be there somewhere. But what would she do? Spot them and confirm their treachery? Ride madly to the camp and shout it from the rooftops? At least it was a plan.

The horse was a wonder. Holly had never experienced a smoother full gallop. But she rode English-style, which made her rise off the saddle. After a couple miles her thighs were burning. At one point the black horse jumped a ravine Holly hadn't seen coming. She stayed on the horse only because she was up out of the saddle and her legs took the shock when her mount landed on the other side. Otherwise she would have tumbled off the horse at a speed known to few people. And it would be a good long time before her broken body was found.

Holly was relieved to reach the trail. The horse had got her there in no more than ten minutes. She sat in the saddle and rested her throbbing thighs. Nothing was in sight but a freight wagon coming up the trail from the south. It traveled toward the camp alone. Now what would she do?

Oh God above, please help me. Courage isn't enough. Holly watched the freight wagon slowly approach, raising dust. Far south of the freight wagon, a cloud of billowing dust told her something else approached on the trail. *Many wagons and riders go south on the trail all day long,* she thought.

"How could I be so foolish?" she complained aloud. "No one would meet right on the trail. There is too much traffic. No one could make any kind of crooked transaction here."

She rose as high in the stirrups as she could. Her legs quivered like reeds. She turned her head slowly to the east. Nothing broke the grassy horizon but scrubby yucca. The sky was as blue as a baby's eyes.

She squinted to the west. Nothing broke the horizon. But the sky was a muted blue. Was it the angle of the sun? She scanned northwest. The sky was pure blue in that direction. She looked southwest. The sky to the southwest was also pure blue.

"Hey!" boomed a voice from the approaching wagon. "Ain't you far from home, Jim Dandy? Hey, you'd be a woman!"

The driver of the freight wagon was a true man of the wilderness. His face was buried in huge dark bush of a beard. In a way it forced a man to rely on his personality. Holly wondered if this man had any personality to spare. He tugged on the long reins to stop four husky mules.

His jaw dropped. He rubbed his fists in his eyes. He gawked. "You're still there sitting on that black pony. I ain't never seen no woman as purty as you even in them painted pitchers."

Holly pointed straight west. "What's over there, sir?"

The bushy head swiveled to look west. "You ain't going yonder, lady. Oh, if you was lucky, in about four or five miles you would cross the army mail route that runs from the camp southwest to the town of Cheyenne."

"Why would I have to be so lucky?"

The man scratched his beard furiously. He sputtered, "Why, ain't you heard of nothing out here, lady? Why, that's where the mail rider old Charley was killed not more than year or so back. The soldier boys call that creek over yonder 'Dead Man Creek' after poor old Charley."

"Who killed him?"

"Naturally folks say the Lakotas done it."

"But?"

"Why, ma'am, it coulda been Doc Middleton and his band of horse thieves, or stagecoach robbers like Fly Speck Billy and Dirty Doak, or whiskey-runners, or tapped-out miners coming back from the Black Hills or—"

"Or gunrunners?"

"Sure. I don't want to leave nobody out. There's a million perfeck spots over in the ravines of them sawed-off hills to hide a million no-accounts."

Holly scanned the low hills to the west. They were notorious. Did she want to go on? Her very fear told her that she was headed in the right direction. This was a favorite hiding place for the Lakotas and gunrunners and who knew who else.

"Hey, lady, you ain't thinking of going over yonder, are you? If you are, by cracky, I'll just have to get off this wagon and hog-tie you."

"I don't think so."

Holly reined her horse straight west and nudged it into a fast canter so she could sit on the saddle. Her legs were tired. She would just have to risk a sudden ravine that the black horse would jump. Her legs were too tired. She could no longer hear the wagon-driver screaming at her to stop when the horse cantered onto a very rough trail. Wagon tracks were visible. It had not rained since Holly came to the camp, so the tracks could be very old. But she had little choice other than to follow them.

She turned in the saddle and for a moment looked back. The wagon was moving toward the camp. She continued west. Soon she saw the faintest outline of dust to the west above the low hills. Gunrunners and Lakotas could be just over any rise now. She couldn't risk riding up over a crest and bursting upon them. She dismounted. She fell to her knees. Her legs were like rubber. She dropped the reins so the horse would not follow her. She walked shakily ahead on the trail.

Holly sat down facing west and cupped her hands over her ears. Did she hear something beyond those low rises? She thought so. The day was the kind of very hot day that made one pray for a breeze. But not now. She wanted dead silence. She had to hear. And maybe she did hear something.

She heard a sharp noise!

What was it? She heard another. The first sound had been jubilant. The second angry. Men's voices? Or her imagination?

She got up and forced herself to walk back and lead her black horse off the trail. There was a knoll not far away. She would leave the horse behind it. She listened hard while she took the horse there but its hooves plodding across the scrabbly hard clay ground drowned out all other sounds.

She rubbed her thighs before she started walking again. Her fine tan riding pants were dusty. And where she put her hands on the pants her fingers left white chalky marks. Her black boots were dusty too. She wiped her hanky across her face. Suddenly she felt for her cap. It was gone. She could feel the sun burning the top of her head now.

"Oh God, don't let me down now," she prayed aloud as if daring someone to interrupt her talk with God.

She walked well off the trail but parallel to it. She was approaching the first low hill to the west. She remembered talking to Franklin about scouting. Don't ever stand up on a crest or a hill top. She got on her hands and knees and crawled. Sharp clay clods bit her knees and jabbed the palms of her hands. But she was using different muscles. She actually felt stronger.

"Thanks to God," she muttered.

She crawled on. And as she got closer and closer to the hilltop she snaked lower and lower. Did she hear voices? Or was it horses whinnying? It was hard to hear with her body worming through scratchy grass and across scrabbly ground. She remembered rattlesnakes and dismissed the thought. They were too smart to be out in this heat. She felt very hot. In spite of the fear that chilled her. Any moment now she would top the hill. She was sure she heard voices now.

She stopped. She raised her head ever so slowly.

There they were!

They were not one hundred yards away in a low draw between two swales. Lakota warriors were milling around a wagon that had a canvas top like an old prairie schooner. Many ponies were on the far side, beyond the wagon. The warriors were unusually talkative. Holly could understand no more than a few words of the jumbled voices and not enough to get the meaning of their conversation.

In the sea of Lakotas bobbed three hats that only white men wore. The hats were worn by the three men! The three dark filthy men that she still had nightmares about were among the Lakota. The three men looked nervous. Had something gone wrong?

They were slowly backing away from the Lakotas—closer to Holly! She tried to sink lower.

"It weren't supposed to be this way," complained one man.

The man who was their ringleader said, "Just keep calm and keep your hand on your gun."

"A lotta good that'll do me when fifty of these red devils have repeating rifles in their hands," growled the third man.

The first man said, "We was supposed to meet with about ten of them braves—just Bloody Hawk and his bunch."

"Ah, shut up," snapped the ringleader, "Our man's inside the wagon now, stalling them. Maybe he'll hold back the ammo."

Who was inside the wagon? Jonah? Was Jonah there? He must be the one inside the wagon. She wanted to stand up and scream.

"How did that dumb dude get into the transaction?" the first man asked.

"He had the moolah to order the rifles."

At that very moment from the wagon stepped Granville Wiggins III!

Holly was horrified, but at the same time she was overjoyed that it wasn't Jonah. Her selfish prayer was answered. How could she ever have wanted Granville? And now Jonah was not involved. Life was perfect again.

It was time to leave. She must crawl off the hill top and get away. She would ride back to camp.

The Lakotas were shouting. The sounds were too ugly to ignore. What was happening? They were crowding the wagon. A second man stepped out on the wagon seat and held up his hands.

It was Jonah!

Her heart must break.

Suddenly some braves turned. They were looking in her direction.

She was standing up! How had that happened?

Holly stumbled down the hillside. Her legs were dead, but she had to run for her life.

seventeen

Holly heard murderous cries and shouts behind her. She glanced around. One brave was chasing her on foot. He swung a war club. A war club that crushed skulls. And he ran like a whirlwind!

Could she make it to her black horse in time to get away?

Her legs were numb, worse than aching. She had little control of them. She stumbled across the scrabbly ground. Where did she leave the horse? Surely she had run far enough.

There was the knoll! The horse was behind the knoll.

She stumbled toward the knoll. She saw the horse. Its eyes were huge. It started to prance backwards. *Oh please, God, don't let the horse be afraid of me and run away from me. Please God.*

"Take it easy, old boy," she tried to say calmly, fear crawling on her like a snake. She could no longer hear running feet behind her.

She lurched and grabbed the reins!

She swung herself into the saddle. She heard a singing sound worse than the buzz of a wasp. An arrow stuck in the side of the knoll and quivered.

Which way should she go? Her head swarmed with possibilities. She was about two miles west of the main trail from the camp to Sidney. She was about three miles southwest of the camp by the way the crow flies. She didn't even know the terrain if she rode northeast, but it was the shortest way to camp.

The horse spun under her as she wheeled it to the northeast. She kneed the horse into a gallop. Her legs hurt terribly, but she had to rise out of the saddle and jockey the horse faster than it had ever run before. She glanced back. Yes, her killers were coming. A cloud of dust billowed over them. It seemed a thousand braves were screaming and brandishing war clubs and lances!

Arrows sang their songs of death over her shoulder and skittered across the hard ground in front of her. She zigzagged the horse. She didn't want to. It slowed the horse down. But she couldn't help it. She couldn't ride in a straight line.

Every Lakota must be chasing her. Not one stayed with the wagon. They didn't have their rifles yet. Why would they all leave the wagon? The answer stung her like a whip across the face. Every warrior chased her because they had to stop her. It was absolutely essential she not reach the camp. And they would not be satisfied with just stopping her. They had to silence her forever. They were going to kill her!

Oh please, God, spare me. Give my horse wings!

But her brave little horse did not have wings. And she had already run it hard. She looked back. Some of the Lakota warriors were falling back. But some of the Lakota warriors were gaining. The math was dead against her. Only one warrior of so many warriors had to catch her.

She looked ahead. Oh no!

High on the hill in front of her was a horseman. Could it be a soldier? No. It was a Lakota. She was trapped!

Holly reined a sharp turn to the right toward the main trail. Her horse spun, staggered, and pitched forward on its knees. Holly flew through the air. Her palms met the hard ground.

She was on her hands and knees. She was dizzy. Screams and shouts pounded her ears. She shook her head. She straightened up, but remained on her knees. Her legs were dead. She looked up. The lone rider was still silhouetted on the hilltop ahead. He was motionless. He had done nothing. Still he had won. Holly was finished now.

The screams and thundering hooves were almost on top of her. She could feel the war clubs. Her skin crawled with expectation. *Oh please, make it quick. And painless.*

She folded her hands. *Please, God, forgive me for all my sins. My life on earth will soon be over.*

Suddenly there was complete silence.

Was she dead already? No. She blinked her eyes. She pinched her arm. She looked ahead to the hilltop. The lone rider held his arms over his head. His hands were locked together. He made the sign for peace.

"Peace! Sweet peace." she cried.

Holly heard herself sobbing. Hot tears ran down her cheeks. *Thank you, God.* She felt low and humble. This miracle wasn't for her. It was for hundreds of people who would not die today. She cried for joy.

Slowly pony after pony clopped by. A long string of Lakota warriors rode their horses toward the hill. A few stared hate at her. A few gaped in wonder: a woman? The lone rider disappeared behind the crest of the hill. It was all over. The catastrophe had been averted. Holly knew the lone rider rode slowly toward the village. She knew the warriors would follow him to a man. She knew which tepee the lone rider would be sitting in tonight. She knew what he would be doing. Dreaming. Looking to the south. He was the great Lakota warrior.

Holly couldn't feel sorry for him. He had so much more than most people.

"Holly!"

She turned, still on her knees. "Franklin!"

He rode in front of many blue uniforms. His entire Troop A must have been riding behind him. Franklin dismounted, pulled her to her feet, and hugged her.

"Are you all right?" he asked.

"Yes." Then she remembered. The memory ripped her like a knife in the heart. "Jonah isn't. He's a no-good gunrunner. I knew in my head he was. But my heart didn't want to believe it."

"Don't worry about Jonah now. Let's get you back to camp.

My, you look tired and dirty."

"Are there any arrows sticking in me?" She laughed. Oh, it was good to laugh. She laughed again. Yes, it was sweet tonic. Franklin watched her soberly. Did he think she was losing her mind? She grabbed his arm, like Esmeralda would. "I'm all right. Take me home."

"Home?" Franklin grinned.

"Yes, *home.* What are you doing out here anyway?" she asked.

"I hope you're not complaining." He laughed. "My job is to scout out gunrunners."

"Blabby told me that! That's why I told you about Jonah."

"I'm sorry I lied to you earlier today. I just thought you would stay at the cottage and keep out of danger. I didn't realize how brave you are. I was going to explain later. Now it's later. I'm sorry."

"You're forgiven," she said as he helped her mount a fresh horse. She blurted, "Oh, please take care of that wonderful black horse." She looked for the horse. It was on its feet and a soldier held the lead to its halter. "Oh, how I would love to own that wonderful little horse. I practically owe it my life."

"Maybe it can be arranged." Franklin smiled as if at a private joke. He mounted his big Appaloosa and waved Troop A to the east. He urged his horse beyond a trot into a canter.

In a canter, Holly could sit the saddle hard and rest her legs. After a few minutes of riding toward the main trail, she felt strong again. She rode close to Franklin. When they reached the main trail, Franklin slowed down and waved the rest of Troop A on to camp. He moved away from the formation of riders and their cantering horses.

He explained to Holly, "We'll walk our horses in. Besides, we can talk better this way."

"Good. Are you going to tell me what happened back there?"

"It was an undercover operation for the army. My troop was back in the hills. We were going to surround the gunrunners and Bloody Hawk's bunch during the transaction. But somehow the word got out in the village and dozens of warriors showed up to make sure they got one of the new repeating rifles. We were going to jump them before the rifles were passed out. But they kept coming until they were so strong we were in a quandary about what to do. It looked like a bloody battle was inevitable."

"How horrible."

"Then a certain young lady showed up and was just the distraction that we needed. They had no time for rifles then. They had to catch you."

"Do you mean I helped the situation?"

"You probably saved the lives of a hundred men today."

"I didn't do it alone."

"That's true. How in the world did Crazy Horse get there when he did? It was a miracle."

Holly almost said, I asked him to come, but stopped. She said, "Yes. It was a miracle. Praise God for that."

She watched Troop A ride by. Granville rode a horse between two soldiers with his hands tied behind his back. He was followed by the three filthy men, each escorted between soldiers. Where was Jonah? She couldn't ask Franklin. She just had to forget Jonah. But she knew Jonah was going to be a painful memory for a very long time.

"How did Granville get into this mess?" she wondered aloud.

"Apparently that letter you mailed to him the first day you came to camp was just too enticing to resist."

"My letter!"

"Yes. You convinced him there were fortunes to be made out in the wilderness and everybody out here was a crook anyway."

"Oh." What else could she say?

"Apparently he has severe financial problems back in Philadelphia. Since his father died, he mismanaged the family's money. Any scheme for quick money was just too tempting for him. Do you remember how he quizzed me about rifles? Well, he already had a shipment of Model 73s on its way from the East. He got to worrying the repeaters were too complicated for these Lakota to operate. That's how little he knew about Indians. Anyway, all he needed was to gain Jonah's confidence and get part of the action. Apparently you told him about Jonah, too."

"Well," she snapped, "I was right, wasn't I?"

Franklin didn't answer her question. "You didn't see Granville for several days, did you?"

"No. I guess not. I saw him Saturday. And I saw him earlier today."

"Today is Wednesday. During those three days you didn't see him, he went to Sidney to bring back his shipment of Model 73s that arrived by railroad. Who would have thought he could have managed that?"

"Greed is inspiring." The subject of Granville irritated her. She felt guilty. "Why are we still waiting here?"

Franklin rose in the stirrups to look back on the trail. "To let another troop pass. Colonel Monroe and two more troops were back in the hills with us. It would have been quite a battle." He smiled at her pleasantly. It was obvious that under the circumstances, Franklin could not be mad at Holly.

Suddenly more troopers thundered past them, headed toward camp. They carried a guidon for Troop D.

Holly asked, "Where is Colonel Monroe?"

"He's with Troop E, bringing in the wagon. Making sure the rifles are protected and accounted for."

She thought about Granville as Troop D continued to ride past. He obviously proposed to her earlier in the day just to shut her up until after the transaction. He wasn't serious. He would have hidden his share of the gold he received as payment from the Lakotas. And then he would have conveniently forgotten the proposal. She made it easy for him to do that by resisting his proposal so strongly. No one would have blamed him for not proposing again. Then one day Granville would have apologetically left the wilderness with his fortune in gold.

Holly felt guilty about Granville. She had gotten to know him too well. She had met his mother, almost. He was humorous. He probably even had a good heart. And the poor weak man who needed money had been tempted by her childish stories. What could she do but pray for him?

A deep ache overwhelmed her. She steadied herself. She wasn't going to ask where Jonah was. But how would she ever forget Jonah? He was the first and only man to kiss her. And deep in her heart she wanted him to be the last man—till death do we part. That was important to her. How could her own heart be so wrong? It told her he was the one. It sang to her. It gave her wings. It heralded love for Jonah.

"All right. Troop D is past." Franklin interrupted Holly's thoughts. "Let's go to camp. You'll probably want to freshen up before you talk to Jonah."

eighteen

"Talk to Jonah?" sputtered Holly.

That was exactly what she didn't want to do. He had betrayed her.

Franklin looked at her expectantly. But he finally smiled and said, "You'll feel better when you've had a chance to rest a while and freshen up. Let's go."

They walked their horses the two miles into camp. Franklin chatted about this and that. He seemed to sense Holly wanted no more heavy conversation. He and Esmeralda were a good match. They were both very sensitive and very civil. Holly had selfishly tried to destroy that—just one more thing she had to regret. It was a good thing God was forgiving.

At the cottage she ate a roast beef sandwich while Franklin and Hop Fong prepared her bath in her bedroom. Then Franklin excused himself.

Holly bathed for a long time. The warm soapy water soothed her. If only it could wash away her heartache for Jonah. Would she ever be able to forget the treachery of her first real sweetheart?

The light was growing dim behind the curtain on her west window. She put on a favorite dress of bottle green watered silk. The mirror reassured her that it was lovely on her. She couldn't resist feeling just for the tiniest moment superior. She found some turquoise earrings that had just the right amount of green to be a perfect match. Papa said he had searched forever to find them.

Holly left her room and walked gracefully to the living room. Franklin glanced up from his chair and smiled his approval. "You look wonderful."

"Thank you. It's really nothing." Ever since her bath, Holly had refused to admit to herself why she wanted to look stunning.

Franklin stood up. "Let's go to the guardhouse."

"All right." While taking her bath, Holly had avoided thinking about the proposed trip to visit Jonah. But deep in her heart, she knew she must go.

The guard escorted Franklin and Holly directly into Jonah's cell. Jonah rose from a bunk and nodded guiltily at Holly. She stayed as far from him as she could in the tiny cell.

Holly looked around. All the other cells were empty. "Where is Granville?" she asked, so she wouldn't have to ask a thousand other questions.

"The colonel is interrogating him in the adjutant's office," answered Franklin. He stepped out of the cell and said to the guard, "Take a half-hour break, Corporal. I'll stand watch here for you."

As soon as the puzzled guard left, Jonah smiled. "Holly, dearest." He reached for her.

"Don't touch me."

Jonah sighed and leaned over to brush off a blanket covering the bunk. "Please sit down," he said.

"For one minute." She sat down reluctantly, glancing at Franklin with irritation.

Jonah looked at Franklin. "Give us a few minutes, Lieutenant."

"Yes, Captain."

"Captain?" exclaimed Holly.

"Shhh." Franklin held one finger to his mouth. He whispered, "No one is supposed to know." Closing the door to Jonah's cell, he walked to the front of the guardhouse and sat in a chair by the door.

Holly was angry. "What did he mean, calling you 'Captain'?"

Jonah smiled. "That's my rank. But only Franklin and the colonel and Esmeralda know that. And now you."

"So I was just a bit player in your big play?" The more the deception sank in, the angrier she became.

"I don't have much time," said Jonah, "so I'll go through everything as objectively as I can."

"Oh. Let's be objective," Holly snapped sarcastically.

He proceeded calmly. "I'm a captain in a special branch of the army. I do undercover work. I've been doing it since 1872. The year before that I was a lieutenant in the 3rd Cavalry in Arizona. In fact Colonel Monroe was there at the time. Fortunately Mrs. Monroe doesn't get around much."

"Maybe she does remember you. I asked her about you at the weekly party and she seemed to remember you at first but then became very evasive."

"She was just being the good army wife."

"Is that what a good army wife does?"

"Among many other wise things. Anyway, Esmeralda certainly remembered me. She gets around a camp a lot—as you know. But that's beside the point. My job here was to assist Franklin in trapping gunrunners by infiltrating them. I've been here a year working on this case. By the way, it was just a fluke that I was the one who brought you to camp from Sidney. But I couldn't get out of it. I was supposed to take the rifles directly to a place near Dead Man Creek south of the camp and hide them with the help of those three men you dislike so much."

"I wondered why Franklin was so nervous about your freight wagon in front of our cottage."

"Our whole plan was in jeopardy because I met you. Somehow you guessed I was in with gunrunners or I was doing something else crooked. Franklin was afraid you would talk about me around the camp and get some of the other officers asking too many questions. My cover required being trusted by the army."

"What are you getting at?"

"Franklin and I decided I must immediately gain your confidence and dispel the bad image you had of me."

"Congratulations. You fooled me."

"I'm not sorry because—"

"You have forged quite a distinguished career fooling people."

"Until a couple weeks ago, I couldn't imagine ever doing anything else."

"And what changed your mind?"

"I fell in love." He knelt on one knee and took her hand.

"Don't start any more treachery, please." Holly's heart was hammering. The cell was spinning. Why had she come here? He had hurt her enough. She tried to stand up.

He pulled her down. "Listen to me. They're moving me out of here at midnight. Everyone is supposed to think I'm being taken to the railroad at Sidney and then sent east to Omaha for trial."

"Where are you going?" Her heart was melting. He really was leaving. There wasn't much time.

"Back to Oregon. I've infiltrated some cutthroats there. They pulled me away from that operation because the situation here was so tense. Oregon is where I got the Appaloosa Franklin rides. It was a gift from the Nez Pierce Indians. After I got here, I realized it was too conspicuous and raised too many questions as to where I had been, so I traded it to Franklin. And he gave me his big bay. I bought the black Arabian for you. But Granville suddenly popped up and I had to let him use it."

"Granville?" Her mind was spinning.

"Don't feel bad about enticing Granville out here. He's so desperate for money, if he hadn't come here for quick money, he would been doing something else illegal."

Holly's mind was reeling. It had bothered her that Jonah hadn't been to church. Now she knew he had to keep a low profile. Some of the odd incidents she'd experienced in the last few weeks now made sense. If only they had the time to leisurely talk about each of them, maybe with a good laugh or two. But she still had a million questions and only time to ask a few. She had to make sure she asked the most important.

"Are you a God-fearing Christian, Jonah Finch?"

"To the core."

"Why must you go?"

"I've infiltrated a lot of whiskey-smuggling, gunrunning, horse-stealing skunks here. If certain ones found out I was really in the army, some of my innocent contacts would get hurt. I must disappear."

"No." She began to cry.

"It would be nice if I could just come out in the open. I could convince you I'm a God-fearing Christian. I could propose to you. And if I were lucky enough to get your approval, we could have a double wedding with Franklin and Esmeralda."

"But—"

"Life isn't that simple. Not for me. Not now."

"I understand," she answered with some bitterness.

"I am proposing, Holly. Will you marry me?"

"But you just said we couldn't."

"Does that mean you won't marry me?" It was the only time she had ever seen fear in his eyes.

"You had better explain first how it can be accomplished."

"I'll get transferred out of this special branch into the regular cavalry as soon as possible," he explained eagerly. "I'm certain they will transfer me quickly. They owe me that much."

"But where would you be transferred?"

"Back to Arizona. There's an Apache there in a lively dispute with settlers. His name is Goyathlay. Some folks call him the Spanish name Geronimo."

"I never heard of him."

"The dispute is getting ugly and that means the army has to step between the belligerents to make peace."

"Before I came west, I would have insisted that statement was a contradiction. Now I know it's true. How does a stubborn Philadelphia girl working with Apache children fit into your plans?"

"Perfect. I'll ask Franklin's permission for your hand tonight. What I have in mind is meeting you and Franklin in San Francisco in a couple months for our wedding, then traveling down to Los Angeles for our honeymoon, then—"

Holly put her finger over his mouth. "No discussion beyond the honeymoon please." She answered the longing in his eyes by whispering, "Yes, I love you, Jonah Finch, if that's your real name."

"My Christian names are Jonah Finch. My surname Lancaster will soon be yours." And without another word, Jonah Finch Lancaster swept Holly into an embrace that told her heart she had found her true home.

A Letter To Our Readers

Dear Reader:

In order that we might better contribute to your reading enjoyment, we would appreciate your taking a few minutes to respond to the following questions. When completed, please return to the following:

Rebecca Germany, Editor
Heartsong Presents
P.O. Box 719
Uhrichsville, Ohio 44683

1. Did you enjoy reading *Love in the Prairie Wilds*?
   ❑ Very much. I would like to see more books
      by this author!
   ❑ Moderately
      I would have enjoyed it more if _____

   _____

2. Are you a member of *Heartsong Presents*? Yes   No
   If no, where did you purchase this book? _____

   _____

3. What influenced your decision to purchase this
   book? (Check those that apply.)

   ❑ Cover   ❑ Back cover copy

   ❑ Title   ❑ Friends

   ❑ Publicity   ❑ Other _____

4. On a scale from 1 (poor) to 10 (superior), please rate the following elements.

___Heroine   ___Plot

___Hero   ___Inspirational theme

___Setting   ___Secondary characters

5. What settings would you like to see covered in *Heartsong Presents* books?

_____

_____

6. What are some inspirational themes you would like to see treated in future books?_____

_____

_____

7. Would you be interested in reading other *Heartsong Presents* titles?   ❑ Yes   ❑ No

8. Please check your age range:
❑ Under 18   ❑ 18-24   ❑ 25-34
❑ 35-45   ❑ 46-55   ❑ Over 55

9. How many hours per week do you read? _____

Name _____

Occupation _____

Address _____

City _____ State _____ Zip _____

Classic Fiction for a New Generation

Pollyanna
and
Pollyanna Grows Up

Eleanor H. Porter's classic stories of an extraordinary girl who saw the good in everyone. . . and made everyone feel good about themselves.

___*Pollyanna*— An orphan dutifully taken in by her repressive aunt, the well-heeled Miss Polly Harrington, Pollyanna Whittier reinvents a game of her father's and finds a way to hide her tears. No one can resist Pollyanna for long and soon almost everyone is playing "the Glad Game," everyone except Aunt Polly. BTP-65 $2.97

___*Pollyanna Grows Up*—Ruth Carew's refined Boston world has just been turned upside down. The reason, of course, is obvious: Pollyanna Whittier has come to visit. From Boston to Beldingsville to Europe and back again, *Pollyanna Grows Up* continues the adventures of an irrepressible American girl on the brink of womanhood at the turn of the century. In everything she does—especially the Glad Game—Pollyanna reflects the boundless love of her Heavenly Father. BTP-80 $2.97

Hearts♥ng

HEARTSONG PRESENTS TITLES AVAILABLE NOW:

(If ordering from this page, please remember to include it with the order form.)

·········Presents·········

*Temporarily out of stock.

Great Inspirational Romance at a Great Price!

Heartsong Presents books are inspirational romances in contemporary and historical settings, designed to give you an enjoyable, spirit-lifting reading experience. You can choose from 132 wonderfully written titles from some of today's best authors like Colleen L. Reece, Brenda Bancroft, Janelle Jamison, and many others.

When ordering quantities less than twelve, above titles are $2.95 each.

SEND TO: Heartsong Presents Reader's Service
P.O. Box 719, Uhrichsville, Ohio 44683

Please send me the items checked above. I am enclosing $_____.
(please add $1.00 to cover postage per order. OH add 6.25% tax. NJ add 6%). Send check or money order, no cash or C.O.D.s, please.
To place a credit card order, call 1-800-847-8270.

NAME _____

ADDRESS _____

CITY/STATE_____ ZIP _____

Hearts♥ng Presents
Love Stories Are Rated G!

That's for godly, gratifying, and of course, great! If you love a thrilling love story, but don't appreciate the sordidness of popular paperback romances, **Heartsong Presents** is for you. In fact, **Heartsong Presents** is the *only inspirational romance book club*, the only one featuring love stories where Christian faith is the primary ingredient in a marriage relationship.

Sign up today to receive your first set of four, never before published Christian romances. Send no money now; you will receive a bill with the first shipment. You may cancel at any time without obligation, and if you aren't completely satisfied with any selection, you may return the books for an immediate refund!

Imagine. . .four new romances every month—two historical, two contemporary—with men and women like you who long to meet the one God has chosen as the love of their lives. . .all for the low price of $9.97 postpaid.

To join, simply complete the coupon below and mail to the address provided. **Heartsong Presents** romances are rated G for another reason: They'll arrive *Godspeed!*